PENGUIN BOOKS

A MOMENT IN TIME

H. E. Bates was born in 1905 at Rushden in Northampton-shire and was educated at Kettering Grammar School. He worked as a journalist and clerk on a local newspaper before publishing his first book, *The Two Sisters*, when he was twenty. In the next fifteen years he acquired a distinguished reputation for his stories about English country life. During the Second World War he was a Squadron Leader in the R.A.F., and some of his stories of service life, *The Greatest People in the World* (1942), *How Sleep the Brave* (1943) and *The Face of England* (1953), were written under the pseudonym 'Flying Officer X'. His subsequent novels of Burma, *The Purple Plain* and *The Jacaranda Tree*, and of India, *The Scarlet Sword*, stemmed directly or indirectly from his war experience in the Eastern theatre of war.

In 1958 his writing took a new direction with the appearance of *The Darling Buds of May*, the first of the popular Larkin family novels, which was followed by *A Breath of French Air*, *When the Green Woods Laugh* and *Oh! To Be in England* (1963). His autobiography appeared in three volumes, *The Vanished World* (1969), *The Blossoming World* (1971) and *The World in Ripeness* (1972). His last works included the novel *The Triple Echo* (1971) and a collection of short stories, *The Song of the Wren* (1972). Perhaps one of his most famous works of fiction is the best-selling novel *Fair Stood the Wind for France* (1944). H. E. Bates also wrote miscellaneous works on gardening, essays on country life, several plays (includ-ing *The Day of Glory*, 1945), *The Modern Short Story* (1941) and a story for children, *The White Admiral* (1968). His works have been translated into sixteen languages. His posthumous collection of stories, *The Yellow Meads of Asphodel*, appeared in 1976.

H. E. Bates was awarded the C.B.E. in 1973 and died in January 1974. He married in 1931 and had four children.

H. E. BATES

A Moment in Time

PENGUIN BOOKS

Penguin Books Ltd, Harmondsworth, Middlesex, England
Penguin Books, 625 Madison Avenue, New York, New York 10022, U.S.A.
Penguin Books Australia Ltd, Ringwood, Victoria, Australia
Penguin Books Canada Ltd, 2801 John Street, Markham, Ontario, Canada L3R 1B4
Penguin Books (N.Z.) Ltd, 182–190 Wairau Road, Auckland 10, New Zealand

—

First published by Michael Joseph 1964
Published in Penguin Books 1967
Reprinted 1969, 1980

—

Copyright © Evensford Productions Ltd, 1964
All rights reserved

—

Made and printed in Great Britain
by C. Nicholls & Company Ltd
Set in Linotype Granjon

Give them their life:
They do not know how short it grows;
So let them go
Young-eyed, steel-fledged, gun-furious,
For if they live they'll live,
As well you know,
Upon the bitter kernels of their sweet ideals.

Give them their wings:
They cannot fly too high or far
To soar above
The dirty-moted, bomb-soured, word-tired world.
And if they die they'll die,
As you should know,
More swiftly, cleanly, star-defined than you will ever feel.

I

'Do come and look, Elizabeth,' my mother said. 'The swans are making a hole in the lake.'

I shall remember for ever, sometimes with joy and pride and at others with sadness and utter dread, but no longer with bitterness, the year 1940, more especially a winter evening deeply entombed in snow, when my mother stood at the big bay window in the drawing-room of our house and said these words to me, in her usual lost and fluttering fashion, as she stared at the lake below. I was then a very young nineteen and I remember, as I started to move over to the window, looking at the illuminated wrist-watch my grandmother had given me for my birthday and seeing that it was exactly five o'clock. It was, though I didn't realize it then, an important moment in time.

My mother was tall and gaunt. Her eyes were dark and never looked well. The skin of her neck was like a piece of chamois leather that had been wrung out and left to dry in brownish, uncomfortable, awkward folds. The flutter in her speech was not so much nervous as indecisive. When she spoke she always seemed to be chasing her words as if they were a brood of re-calcitrant chickens she was trying to get to roost and when she finally spoke to them they were nearly always the wrong ones. Hence the hole in the lake.

'A very big hole?' my grandmother said. She was sitting by the big open fire-place, her skirt up to her knees, her brilliant dark head erect, her legs rosy in the light of a great flaming fire of ash-boughs. In contrast to my mother her voice was firm. Its tone was level, with a certain controlled acidity about it. Her question mocked my mother, but lightly and without cruelty. My mother in any case was quite incapable of being hurt by it for the simple reason that in her absent-minded way she was wholly unaware that the words carried with them any such purpose as mockery. In the same way my grandmother could have flattered her and she wouldn't have been aware of that

7

either. She was a human duck off whose back even the most sereing of words flowed like harmless rain.

I reached the window and stood by her side. After a week of frost and snow the lake had become one with the land. Only a crest or two of frozen reed sticking up through billows of snow marked the line of the banks, beyond which copses of hazel and alder stood like a low petrified forest, the intense whiteness of it fired by the savage carmine ball of the setting sun.

Below us the swans, five of them now, were swimming slowly round and round, occasionally breasting the thick edges of snow and ice, keeping open their clear dark circle of water. My mother, in her funny way, was right after all. It really did look like a big black hole, a bottomless grave in the glistening sepulchral whiteness of snow.

'I could have sworn there were seven of them,' she said.

'There were,' I said, 'yesterday. But they had a great fight. I watched it. The other two were strangers and the five drove them away.'

'That was very cruel,' she said. 'Why couldn't they be sociable.'

'Swans,' my grandmother said, 'have no idea what it is to be sociable.'

'Oh ! don't they ? I always think they look so neighbourly. I suppose it's the shape of them. Did anyone give them bread today ?'

'I gave them bread,' I said, 'three times.'

'That was nice. They look sort of in prison, don't they ?'

Again, in her odd way, she was right. The clear circle of water was their prison. In the great friendly embalming stretch of snow it looked curiously dark and sinister.

'Is there any more toast ?' I said. 'I'm simply ravenous still.'

'We shared the last piece ten minutes ago,' my grandmother said. 'If you really want more ring for Edna.'

'Oh ! I'd love to make it myself. Couldn't I ? I adore making toast by the fire.'

'Ring for Edna.'

The war was still young. The notion of making one's own toast by the fire was, for our family at any rate, still an unthinkable one.

8

I crossed over to the fireplace and pulled the bell-pull and rang for Edna. As if by some sort of magic the door opened instantly and my Uncle Harry came in.

It would be truer to say that he exploded in. He came sweeping in like a big hairy whirlwind. His heavy reddish-brown tweed suit matched his thick coarse hair, which not only came down low over his forehead but sprouted in lush gingery watch-springs from his ears and nostrils. At some distant date, before I was born, he had broken his right leg in a fall from a horse and the resulting lameness caused all his physical acts to be done, as it were, at double strength. The ferocity of his clumsiness was that of an unbalanced bull.

'Tea finished? Doesn't matter. I'll have a whisky-and-soda.'

In the act of pouring himself a whisky and soda at the table by the window he twice dropped the stopper of the decanter and once spouted soda on to the carpet. At the first of these explosions I actually saw my mother jump. At the third she merely crept away, after the fashion of a whipped dog, and sat down on a low claret-coloured needlework chair away from the fire.

'They say whisky's going to be damn scarce. Any toast left?'

'We're just about to ask for some,' my grandmother said.

The soda siphon, suddenly caught by a ponderous elbow, spun like a lop-sided top on the polished surface of the table. My Uncle Harry, grabbing at it with a meaty hand, promptly bashed it over.

'I occasionally wonder,' my grandmother said, 'why you don't use a hammer and chisel for mixing your drinks.'

That the arrow of her words was too subtle for him hardly mattered. A moment later Edna knocked on the door. My grandmother called for her to come in and presently she was in the room, a thin, grey-haired, round-shouldered woman, half at attention and dressed in black, with white lace cap and apron. I had once heard my Uncle Harry call her – not in the presence of my grandmother – 'ninepenny worth of scrag-end,' and the description, rather like some of my mother's, was an oddly apt one. There was more bone than flesh on Edna and such bone as there was seemed to creak as she limped along.

'You rang, ma'am?'

'Of course she rang,' my Uncle Harry said. 'If she didn't ring why are you here?'

'Bring toast for two, please, Edna,' my grandmother said.

It seemed to me that Edna trembled. Her already ash-pale face seemed to grow whiter. I was still trying to wonder why a simple request for toast should have had this devastating effect on her when she actually said:

'I'm sorry, ma'am. I can't.'

'What do you mean, you can't?'

'We've no bread, ma'am.'

'Good grief,' Harry said. '*No what?*'

'Bread, sir. The baker couldn't get through today. Nor yesterday.'

'Stale will do perfectly well for toast,' my grandmother said. 'Haven't you any stale?'

'No, ma'am. Miss Elizabeth threw the last of the stale to the swans.'

At this shattering announcement my Uncle Harry's mouth dropped open, as if either in the beginning of prayer or protest, but not a sound emerged.

'If there's no toast I'll have a piece of my birthday cake,' I said.

'Yes, miss. Will that be all, ma'am?'

'That will be all, Edna. Thank you.'

Edna backed dumbly out of the room. The door hadn't been shut more than ten seconds before my grandmother whipped herself to her feet, turned on Harry and said in a seething voice:

'I will not have Edna spoken to in that fashion. What in Heaven's name has got into you?'

'I – I –'

'Don't slobber,' Some few drops of whisky and soda had fallen from my Uncle Harry's lips in the course of a brief mono-syllabic protest. 'And don't say it's the war getting on your nerves. I've heard that before.'

'I had a row with that beggar Mitchell. I threatened to sack him.'

'Then you'd better threaten to unsack him. What was the reason for this magnanimous gesture?'

'I told him to dig the snow away from the gates. The drifts

are all of twelve foot deep there. He went damned insolent all of a sudden and said he had only one pair of hands.'

'You could have made them four.'

'I've been cleaning my guns.'

'To shoot what? The approaching enemy?'

'There are still a good few wild duck. I thought of going out tomorrow.'

My mother, woken as if out of a dream, now uttered the first words she had spoken since the shattering episode of the decanter. As usual they were strangely mixed and wrong and yet right at the same time.

'I don't think,' she said, 'wild duck ought to be shot while the Red Cross are so desperate for things.'

'I suppose if we keep them alive they'll drive ambulances,' my grandmother said. 'Is that it?'

Suddenly, as if this part of the conversation had never taken place, my mother said in her fluttering, amiable way:

'Mr Hudson always clears the snow away. He always brings the snow-plough.'

My Uncle Harry went over to the fire and kicked an ash-log into flame. Ash, they always say, burns like a candle and suddenly it was as if the whole room became filled with a great glow of candlelight. The reflection of the brilliant yellow flares on the darkening lake outside startled me and I almost expected to see the swans, startled too, get up and fly away. But when I looked down again they were still there, swimming round and round in the twilight, imprisoned in their clear sinister ring of water.

'That's another damn fine thing,' Harry said. 'Where's the snow-plough? Days and days of snow and no snow-plough. Nothing ever gets done since this damn war started.'

'Started?' I said. 'When did it start?'

This bright remark of mine drew no comment from anyone; nor did its empty triviality, together with that of the rest of the conversation, strike me at the time. I remember, on the other hand, thinking that the business of the bread was very bad. There really ought to have been bread. There was no excuse for that. The baker really ought to have got through. And the snow-plough too. I thought Harry was right about the snow-plough.

My grandmother suddenly went back to the fire to warm her knees, ending her acid attack on Harry as swiftly as it had begun. She might well have sensed the return of Edna, who in fact knocked on the door some few seconds later and came into the room bearing the remaining half of my birthday cake, together with a plate and a silver cake knife, on a *papiermâché* tray.

'Oh! good,' I said. 'I'm raging ravenous.'

My school-girl words and crow of delight were as trivial as my remark about the start of war had been. After I had made it Edna put the tray on a little walnut side-table and asked me if I would cut the cake myself or if I would rather she cut it for me?

'Oh! you cut it,' I said. 'And a good big old wedge too.'

Edna, having cut a thick dark segment of cake, then stood decorously by the door, hands folded in front of her apron.

'Yes, Edna?' my grandmother said. 'Did you wish to say something?'

'Mr Hudson has called, ma'am.'

'Which Mr Hudson, Edna? Young or old?'

'The young one, ma'am. He would very much like to speak to you.'

'Ah! the jolly old snow-plough johnny,' Harry said. 'And about time too.'

My grandmother instantly gave him a glare so brilliant with the reflection of ash-flame that he shut himself up immediately, mouth first dropping open and then closing again like a trap.

'Show Mr Hudson in.'

For some reason or other I suddenly felt unaccountably shy. The evening was rapidly growing darker every moment but when my grandmother suddenly asked Harry to switch on the lights I immediately begged him not to.

'Oh! no. Not yet. Let's keep the firelight. The firelight's so beautiful.'

So we kept the firelight. If the swans were imprisoned in their ring of water I now felt equally imprisoned by the bright ring of ash-flame. I stood withdrawn against the big bay window and for the next several minutes – there might equally well have been five or fifty of them for all I knew – I didn't speak a word except to say 'Good-evening' when Tom Hudson came.

Tom was a big, fair, muscular boy of twenty who, I now saw, was wearing glasses. I had never seen him in glasses before and it made him seem suddenly very much of a stranger. Something about the glasses seemed to make him nervous too and for the most of the time he kept rolling a pair of big sheep-skin gloves round and round in his hands.

He began by saying he'd come to apologize about the snow-plough. He was very sorry about the snow-plough. His tractor had broken down. But everything was in order now and if all went well he would be out at first light tomorrow, getting the roads clear.

During the course of his saying all this Uncle Harry broke in to offer him a whisky and soda but he refused, out of sheer nervousness I thought. And presently, nervousness being infectious, I started to feel impossibly nervous too. It wasn't that Tom was a stranger to me. His father had farmed a hundred and fifty acres of our land on the far side of the lake for as long as I could remember. As a child I had ridden on hay carts with him and as a girl I had ridden side by side with him at hunt meetings. When we met we called each other by Christian names.

The growing feeling that something about him was wrong this evening, in some way disjointed, was suddenly confirmed by a remark of my grandmother's. She, in her shrewd way, had sensed it too.

'Tom, do forgive me if I seem exceptionally personal but I don't ever recall seeing you in glasses before.'

'That's right. I've only just had them.'

From the way he said this – he sort of tried to throw the words away, over-casually – it might have been that he was ashamed of the glasses. The fact of them was a physical humiliation.

'Your eyes,' my grandmother said, 'always look so bright and healthy.'

'Blue eyes always do,' my mother said.

'I went to join up,' Tom said. 'Air Force. They turned me down because of the eyes. Not a hope, they said.'

'Ah! well,' Uncle Harry said. 'We'll need grub. We'll need you on the land. Every bit as important.'

As if these few words solved not only Tom Hudson's problems but those of the war in general, Uncle Harry went over to the fireplace and started to bash about with his pipe, hammering it first on the heel of his shoe, then on the bricks of the hearth and finally digging noisily at it with his knife. The racket of all this apparently not being enough he then took a running kick with his good leg at an ash-bough, knocked it clean off the fire and then threw a fresh one at it, scattering wood-ash everywhere and generating more sparks than any anvil.

Fresh flames shot into the air. The room was as bright as day. I saw my grandmother scowl and then Tom Hudson said:

'I'm sorry, but isn't it about time for black-out?'

'Good grief,' Uncle Harry said. 'I'm always forgetting.'

He stumped across to the window. I stepped aside. The big bay had been difficult to screen. Ten inch strips of black paper were pasted round the edges of the glass. The heavy crimson velvet curtains were thickly lined with black too and as Uncle Harry wrenched at them there was a mad overhead jangling of brass rings on the curtain pole.

'I suppose you want to drive one of those things up there?' Uncle Harry said. He now proceeded to switch on the lights, once again crashing into the soda siphon in his thumping course across the room. 'Fighters or bombers?'

'Is there a difference?' my mother said.

Even I winced at this, though I hadn't the vaguest idea what the difference was either.

'Fighters,' Tom said. I thought he seemed acutely embarrassed, under the revealing glare of electric light, by the whole affair. I thought it also seemed impossible that his very bright blue eyes were any sort of handicap and they merely looked restless as he said: 'Tony Jackson's in fighters. He was home from France the other day. Went back yesterday.'

'Not young Johnson from Egerton Court?' my grandmother said. 'Robert Johnson's son?'

'Yes. Seems impossible that he's only ten minutes flying time away.'

'But he's only a boy,' my mother said. 'He doesn't look strong enough.'

'He was telling me about a fight he had not long ago. He and a Hun just went round and round, glaring coldly at each other before he shot him down.'

'Good grief,' Uncle Harry said. 'He always looked a bit of a dreamer.'

I suddenly felt as if I were in a dream too. It wasn't merely that the aspect of war suddenly presented by Tom Hudson was unreal. The war seemed unreal anyway. I was a girl and I wasn't part of it. It was outside of me somewhere and I didn't understand it. It didn't seem necessary for me to understand it either.

'Of course they just hate this snow. They just long for the spring. He says there'll be fun and games in the spring.'

I found myself listening uneasily. Into the woolly recesses of my dreamy vacuum there slowly penetrated the delayed echo of his voice. It was strangely full of longing. It was also painfully youthful and perhaps for that reason I was embarrassed too.

Later that same year I was to hear that same echo, in varying degrees, in other voices, but that evening I didn't know this. As I look back on it I realize that everything, in spite of the extraordinary sharpness of my memories now, was very vague. I suppose the best way of putting it is to say that I really wasn't awake. Even that doesn't quite explain my feeling of being immersed in unreality, partly shut away.

Presently Tom Hudson stopped fidgeting with his gloves, put them down on the back of the chair, turned up the collar of his overcoat and said he ought to be going. 'Have one for the road?' Uncle Harry said. Tom thanked him, shook his head and said he wouldn't really. He had the tractor outside. He had a feeling it was going to snow again.

Then he started to say good night to us, first to my grandmother, then my mother, then to Uncle Harry and finally to me. Between the first of these good nights he interposed to tell us once again that he would be back with the snow-plough, early, the following morning. He said he would try to clear the whole of our avenue for us, from the front door to the gates at the road. The double line of horse chestnuts, about a hundred and fifty yards long, had been pollarded the previous winter, more for safety than anything else, after three massive boughs had split and fallen in a gale, and now they looked strange and gaunt in the snow, like objects from a slightly sinister fairy tale.

'Have you a torch?' my grandmother said. 'It must be quite dark now.'

Up to that moment he had been altogether very serious but now he smiled, for the first time.

'Funny thing,' he said, 'my eyes are all right in the dark.'

With that he turned and said good night to me. His eyes were briefly but directly focused on me and he used my Christian name. It wasn't the first time he had used it by any means but suddenly for the one and only time that evening the feeling of vagueness left me. I stepped momentarily out of my vacuum. So much was I awake suddenly that I actually smiled back at him, at the same time lifting one hand and throwing back a loose strand or two of my hair.

'Good night, everyone,' he said.

'See Mr Hudson out, Elizabeth,' my grandmother said.

'Oh! no, no. Please. I'll manage. I can find my way.' he said and in a hurried burst of embarrassment was gone.

The ensuing two or three minutes were largely taken up by Uncle Harry starting an untidy personal conflagration with his pipe. Matches were too simple a medium for the purpose and special yellow and crimson spills, which he got from some shop in Bond Street, had to be used instead. The room filled rapidly with smoke. Harry struck with a heavy boot at the heart of the fire, rousing it into flame and saying how cold the night was. My grandmother scowled again and said it was time for a glass of sherry and would Harry stop rampaging about and be good enough to get it for her? Harry blundered across the room like a hippopotamus, finally fetching up against the chair by which Tom Hudson had stood.

'Good grief, young Hudson's left a glove.'

'I'll take it,' I said. 'He can't have got far.'

I snatched up the glove and went out of the room and down the long tiled dimly-lit hall to the front door. It was very chilly in the hall and harshly, bitterly cold as I opened the door. A row of icicles like the crystal drops of a chandelier hung from the roof of the porch and beyond them I could just make out the spectral black outlines of the first of the pollarded chestnuts. 'Tom!' I called and waved the glove. It was an utterly useless gesture and in another instant my voice froze on the snowy darkness.

Far beyond the avenue gates a searchlight, and then a second and a third, threw faint swinging foolscaps of light to the stars. I thought for a moment I heard the sound of a plane. In time I remembered the black-out and pushed the door shut behind me. Then I realized that what I could hear was the sound of a tractor driving away down the road and suddenly, in a strange moment of utter isolation, I was overcome by the oppressive notion that for some reason I was never going to see Tom Hudson again.

It was a notion that couldn't have been more wrong but it was enough to drive me, shivering, back into the house. In that moment all the unreality of war encompassed me completely again and presently, still carrying the glove, I was back with my grandmother, my mother and Harry, imprisoned with them as securely as the swans were imprisoned by their dark ring of water.

2

OFTEN, in the late winter, we heard the ghostly growl of distant artillery fire. It seemed always to come from the direction of the sea. We were not more than twenty miles from the sea in a straight line but the fact merely seemed to increase, rather than lessen, the unreality of the gunfire. We also heard, almost every day, the sound of air-raid sirens but the wails no longer drove us to the cellar, where six months or more before my mother had been accustomed to sit for hours in breathless and dreadful tension while my grandmother played ice-calm games of patience and Harry moodily swigged at his whisky.

The cold left us very reluctantly. A long succession of white savage weeks brought us to a March in which there was no sign of spring. The banks of the lake were still wrapped in white marble waves. Bitter winds rattled the dry reeds and always when the swans took to flight you heard the strange whine of their passage, like the wind's echo.

All at once summer began in April. Orchards suddenly offered a rich and shining feast of plum bloom. In sheets of almost unbearably brilliant emerald young wheat rose from under the snow and soon primroses, together with crowds of white anemones, spread themselves everywhere about the copses, the lakeside and the banks of the little river where Harry had already started to cast for trout. It was really warm at last and there was a great chorus of bird-song everywhere.

In this new idyllic atmosphere I woke late one morning, had my bath and then, looking out of my bedroom window, saw my grandmother in the paved courtyard below. She was talking to two men. They were wearing blue uniforms and peaked caps of the same colour and one of the caps was resplendent with thick gold braid.

My grandmother looked dominant and peremptory. Her head was high. It was a very fine head in any circumstance, with its wide arresting forehead and exceptionally bright black hair, but that morning, in the brilliant April sun, it looked positively queenly. She looked like a woman half her age.

All at once it struck me that her manner wasn't merely peremptory. She was stiff with anger. The fact that she hardly made a single gesture as I stood there watching her merely increased the magnificence of her tension. I couldn't think for the life of me what it was all about but after watching for another minute or two I dressed hurriedly and started to go downstairs.

At the head of the staircase I was passed by a glassy-eyed figure who half-fell up the last three steps and then staggered blindly past me, stuttering out the frozen words :

'We must pack. We've got to pack.'

It was my mother. With another broken cry she disappeared into her bedroom.

The staircase, built of heavy oak, was splendid and wide. My grandmother was intensely proud of it. Rich carvings of grapes, wheat ears, roses and water-lilies – all, I suppose, symbolic of the bountiful countryside surrounding us – adorned the head and foot of it. But that morning, as I groped my confused way down it, I felt it seemed curiously barren. Vague as my mother, I felt a sense of doom.

In the hall below I bumped into Harry, or rather Harry, even more clumsily directionless than usual, bumped into me.

'What on earth,' I said, 'is happening?'

He barged against the door of his study, crashing it open.

'Requisitioning the place.'

'Requisitioning? What? Who?'

'Air Force johnnies. I've got to ring Partridge.'

Partridge was the family solicitor. With a further crash but no further word of explanation Harry disappeared.

I went outside, into the courtyard. The two Air Force officers, preceded by the rigid figure of my grandmother, were coming towards the house. The elder of the two, the one with gold braid on his cap, was rather rubicund. He looked, I thought, something like a sea-dog of Drake's time; there was something robustly Elizabethan about him. The other was taller and slighter. He sported a tremendous barley-eared moustache, the colour of dark sherry.

I suddenly felt intensely shy. I half-turned to scurry away but my grandmother halted me in a voice that I can best describe as salty. But that I mean that it somehow sounded dry, white and bitter.

'Don't go, Elizabeth. I'm sure you will be most interested in what these gentlemen have just said to me. This is my grand-daughter, Elizabeth. Elizabeth, this is Group Captain –'

The two officers saluted me. I felt myself blushing and their names were lost on me.

'They are proposing,' my grandmother said, again in that salty voice, 'to take the house away from us.'

'Now that isn't quite true, Mrs Cartwright.'

My grandmother turned on the elder of the two officers with a look of regal scorn.

'Are you suggesting I am suddenly hard of hearing? If it isn't what you propose then what do you propose?'

'I said that we were looking for a house for use as an extra Officers' Mess. This is the sort of house we're looking for and I think we should like to take it over.'

'And by what authority?'

'We have every authority, madam, as I explained before.'

'And who delegates authority to rob people of their property?'

'There is a war on, madam.'

'I am perfectly well aware of it.' She gave the two officers, their caps and the white wings above their breast pockets calm and separate glares of scorn. The elder of the two officers had a double row of brilliant medal ribbons across his chest and she reserved yet another separate glare for them too, her eyes flashing like magnifying glasses. 'And I might add that since there is a war on I regard it as your duty to protect us, not to fleece us of our rights and privileges and property.'

'Even an Air Force flies on its stomach.'

'So you propose to descend on us like' – she waved a contemptuous, regal arm – 'like an army of locusts and strip us bare!'

'We –'

'My family has lived in this house for four hundred years. Even Cromwell couldn't turn us out. And what Cromwell couldn't do I'm certain no one else is going to do.'

'I very much hope you will see sense and reason about this, Mrs Cartwright. I hope you will co-operate.'

'I have every intention of doing so.' All of a sudden she gave him the most disarming of smiles. 'Perhaps you and your colleague will come in and have a glass of sherry?'

The officers half-bowed their thanks. The four of us went into the house. On the way the elder of the officers ran his hand in silent approbation over the carvings at the foot of the stairs and my grandmother noted it acidly.

In the big drawing-room she herself poured out the sherry. I withdrew to the window and stared at the lake below. Many new water-lily leaves covered the surface of it now and the sun was brilliant on the gold-green circles of them. On the near bank a pair of swans were nesting, not twenty yards from where, in winter, they had kept open their iceless ring of water, and I could see the cob, the male, majestically swimming about the same circle, wings slightly aggressive, watching for intruders.

'Is the lake very deep?'

I turned to find the younger of the officers standing at my side. I found his physical presence intensely disturbing and merely said:

'Oh! I believe so. In places.'

'Looks wizard. Tempting to go in for a swim.'

Wizard? Curious word, I thought, and said:

'You wouldn't make a stroke. The swan would see to that.'

'Oh! so the swan resents us too.'

'I didn't say I resented you.'

'No? Awfully sorry.'

He ran an over-polite and consequently rather mocking hand across the barley-ears of the moustache, so that I felt even more disturbed.

A moment later Harry exploded into the room with the shattering news that Partridge was out of town for two or three days and that we were all ruddy well done like dinners. My grandmother greeted this last expression with a withering stare that halted even Harry, though not for long. He had clearly been working up a private rage of his own and now suddenly shook his fist at the elder of the officers and half-shouted:

'You won't get away with this, I tell you! You won't get away with it!'

'We are not trying to get away with anything, sir. But if Air

Ministry decides to requisition this property then it will have to be requisitioned.'

'You damn well won't get away with it, I tell you!'

Suddenly I was powerfully struck by the fact that Harry in his civilian clothes looked bloated, untidy, shabby and in some curious way unmanly. Beside the well-pressed uniforms of the two officers his baggy tweeds looked horribly and hopelessly wrong.

'You said something just now about *if* Air Ministry decided,' my grandmother said. 'Does that mean there is some uncertainty?'

'Frankly, Mrs Cartwright, no. We desperately need more room. We must have it.'

'Haven't I some right of appeal in this?'

'I'm afraid there isn't time. We need the house in forty-eight hours.'

'Good God! Good grief!' Harry said.

'You mean you would turn me out of my home in two days?' my grandmother said. 'Just like that? I never heard of anything so brutal.'

'War is rather apt to be brutal.'

'I've always understood it also had its decencies.'

The officer said nothing. I felt sick. Harry did a complete blundering circle of the room and finally fetched up by the window, hammering his fist on the frame.

'And where,' my grandmother said, 'do you suppose we are going to live?'

'That's something I'm afraid I can't arrange, madam. I wish I could. I know it's all very painful for you —'

'Painful.' Even she, in that moment, looked utterly bewildered. The one word, neither question nor protest, was full of despair. I was full of despair too and suddenly said what I suppose must have sounded like an exceedingly puerile and stupid thing:

'But you can't do such a thing. It will kill her.'

Instantly she was her old self again.

'I'm not so easily killed, thank you.'

'My adjutant is due back from leave this afternoon,' the

Group Captain said. 'I will send him and Flight-Lieutenant Ogilvy over to arrange final details.'

I saw my grandmother wince at the word final but beyond that, in her stiff way, she showed no sign of further emotion.

'I suppose we get some ruddy pittance for letting the place, eh?' Harry said. 'And what about damage? There'll be a hell of a lot of careless bastards rampaging all over the place I suppose. What about that?'

The Group-Captain clearly didn't like the word bastards and it was now his turn to be stiff.

'I said, sir, that the house was for use as an *Officers'* Mess.'

Harry had no word of answer and the Group-Captain, with a cold gesture, turned to my grandmother.

'That's a very magnificent staircase you've got, Mrs. Cartwright. I'll have it boxed in.'

She thanked him, acidly. Oh! yes, it was very good of him, really very considerate, to think of the staircase.

'You couldn't by any chance box us in? Or spare us an inch or two of attic?'

'I think we must go, Mrs Cartwright. Thank you very much for the sherry.'

Half a minute later the revolution was over. Harry stormed back to his study and my grandmother stood with deceptive calm by the window, arms folded, looking out. I wanted desperately to say something to comfort her but there was a great lump in my throat and I knew very well I should cry if I started to speak.

Instead I went upstairs. On the landing a door opened and was banged shut again. It was my mother once more and this time she greeted me with the tearful, fluttering announcement 'I shall go to Malvern! I shall go to Malvern!' as if that hilly haven of refuge were heaven itself.

That afternoon I walked slowly along the lake and then along the banks of the little river that fed into it at the southern end. There were woods for half a mile along one side of the river and you could smell the deep glorious scent of the first bluebells.

I longed desperately, that afternoon, to talk to someone; but that wasn't all. I longed desperately to talk to someone of my own generation. The revolution of the morning had had a curious effect on me. With alarming clarity I suddenly saw my mother as a figure of pitiful futility and Harry hardly less so. What was more I felt I saw my grandmother with something like adult objectivity for the first time. She seemed to me almost like some female Canute, trying to stem the waters of war.

But what had affected me most was that brief and not exactly pleasant interview with the younger of the two officers, by the window. I was, as I have said, a very young nineteen and I suppose I fancied that what I had said about the swans was very clever. Now I had already started to regret it. I would have given anything to have been able to make some sort of redress.

There was another thing. Although I wasn't fully aware of it at the time I was already on the verge of an attack, and a very bad one, of hero worship. The intense physical disturbance of the morning had become amazingly persistent. I couldn't get those handsome, barley-eared moustaches out of my mind.

Two hundred yards along the river there was a small white bridge that led to a path through the woods that, in turn, led to the land the Hudsons farmed. I started walking through the woods and heard, presently, the sound of a tractor. When I came out of the woods I could see Tom Hudson chain-harrowing the field beyond. After a minute or so he saw me and waved his hand and I waved in answer.

Then he drove the tractor over to me and stopped it and said hullo and what a beautiful day it was. For some unaccountable reason I suddenly started feeling mightily superior and said :

'I hoped I'd see you. I've got some rather terrific news.'

'Oh?' he said. 'Peace been declared or something?'

This frivolous remark rather set me on edge.

'Not exactly. The Air Force is going to requisition the house. Our house, I mean. For an officers' Mess.'

'Good God. Amazing thing.'

'Why amazing? Even an air force flies on its stomach.'

I said this as if it were some highly original remark I'd thought up on my own.

'You mean they're actually turning you out?'

'They are. And in forty-eight hours.'

'But where on earth will you live?'

'Mother's moving to Malvern to live with Aunt Rosemary, and my grandmother and Harry and I are moving into the bailiff's house.'

'Good God. I think that's pretty rough.'

'Oh! do you?' I said. 'I think it's rather wizard.'

I aired the word wizard with what I thought was splendid nonchalance and he looked very hard at me.

'Of course grandmother's terribly upset and mother's in floods of tears and Uncle Harry's bouncing about like a lunatic but after all you've got to see it the other way.'

'The other way?'

'The officers, I mean. The Air Force. Oh! we had two officers over all morning. Absolutely charming, both of them. I had a long talk with one of them and after what he said I must say I rather saw it their way.'

My despicable part in this conversation wasn't exactly deliberate. Perhaps it was merely my way of rationalizing the situation. I don't quite know. But the words came out as if premeditated. Moreover I was so young and impervious and obtuse that it didn't ever occur to me remotely that I might be causing him pain. I had utterly forgotten the desperation of his disappointment about the eyes.

For a moment or two longer he looked rather crushed. He was wearing an open-necked blue shirt and an old pair of yellowish corduroys and I remember suddenly thinking the same thing about him as I had thought about Harry — that the civilian dress looked untidy and shabby and somehow all wrong.

'What about moving the furniture and all the stuff?' he said presently. 'If it's any help I'll bring the tractor over.'

'Oh! I think that's all arranged,' I said. 'Well, I must go now. Two of the officers are coming over again about four o'clock and I rather want to be there. It's all rather exciting.'

'Yes,' he said.

As I turned, tossing my hair back, I had a final glimpse of him sitting steadfastly on the tractor, the large blue eyes transfixed behind his spectacles, and again it didn't occur to me that he might have been in pain.

The courtyard of the house has a stone balustrade running

along one side of it; from it there is a drop of six feet or so to a long bed of roses, beyond which a lawn slopes down to the lake edge. I was walking rather dreamily along this lawn on my way home that afternoon, not really taking much notice of anything, when a voice said:

'Careful of the swan.'

Very startled, I looked up to the balustrade and there were the barley-eared moustaches leaning over.

'My goodness,' I said, 'you frightened the life out of me.'

'Sorry. Came at you out of the sun.'

I couldn't think what on earth this curious expression meant and he gave no hint of an explanation but merely grinned. It was a very engaging grin and he followed it by saying:

'Glad I saw you. Fancy I put up a bit of a black this morning.'

I couldn't think what on earth that meant either and I merely said 'Oh?'

'The bit about the swan, I mean. I thought you took rather a dim view.'

I might have been listening to a foreign language. I stared, open-mouthed, and he said:

'I suppose the business about the house and all that rather shook you.'

'We didn't find it exactly pleasant.'

'Oh! I say. *We* are *not* amused.'

Before I could think of a reply to this he suddenly did an extraordinary thing. He put one hand on the balustrade and with the ease of a circus performer vaulted clean over it and landed at my feet. He then gave a cheeky sort of mock salute and said:

'O for Ogilvy presents his compliments, ma'am, and begs permission to make amends – if that's the right phrase, which I doubt.'

He spread out his arms and for one awful moment I thought he was about to take me in his embrace and kiss me. I felt and must have looked absolutely stony. No one had ever behaved to me in this astounding fashion before and my emotions were somewhere between excitement and outrage.

'Oh! don't look at me like that, please. I can't be as bad as all that, for Pete's sake. Am I really in disgrace with fortune and men's eyes?'

He made a sudden grimace of mock pain and I tried, in turn, to look as dignified as possible.

'Shall I call you Liz, Lizzie, Liza, Elizabeth, Beth, Betty, Bess or plain ma'am? State the alternative preferred, with reasons for your choice.'

'I'm not sure I want you to call me anything.'

At this he made another mock gesture, at the same time sweeping a hand across those magnificent moustaches, and said:

'You know, I rather think I shall have to introduce you to Chloe.'

I was foolish enough to ask who Chloe was and he said:

'Ah! who is Chloe? What is she, that all her swains commend her? Wizard job, Chloe. If you can spare the time I'll introduce you.'

'Can *you* spare the time?' I said. 'I thought you came over to make arrangements about the house.'

'Oh! the Adj is doing that. That's his pigeon.'

We started walking. I was half way to being in a flat spin, as I should have called it only a little later, and I was hardly conscious of mounting the steps that led to the courtyard or of crossing the courtyard into the avenue beyond, where the double row of pollarded chestnuts were now sprouting fresh short growths of the vividest April green.

There we halted. Why I remembered it at that particular moment I don't know, but suddenly I recalled the snow. For a few seconds it imprisoned me again, so that I only half heard him say:

'Liz – Chloe. Chloe – Liz.'

I woke to see him patting with elaborate affection the bonnet of the oldest and oddest little two-seater sports job I had ever seen. Chloe had been done over in yellow and black and looked something like an enlarged tin wasp with eyes – her headlamps – out of all proportion to her size.

I suppose there is nothing quite so infectious as banter and already I was learning fast from Bill Ogilvy.

'Does it actually go?' I said.

'*It? It?* Oh! what a wounding thing to say.'

'My apologies.'

'Offer them to Chloe. She's highly sensitive in these matters. Highly sensitive.'

'How old is she?'

'Hell!' he said. 'How *what*? – Age cannot wither nor custom stale – Oh! Liz, Liz – please, please.' All of a sudden he wrenched open the door of the car. 'Hop in!'

'No thanks,' I said. 'I don't want to be killed. I'm too young.'

'Madam, I beg you. I entreat. Prithee,' he said and suddenly, with a gracious bow, lightly held my hand.

It was utterly impossible to resist these charming blandishments and I got into the car. Several seconds later a major explosion tore the air and we were away down the chestnut avenue like a yellow sky-rocket, my black hair streaming out in the wind.

At the end of the avenue we skidded out into the road with a calamitous scream of tyres and a white blast of dust. Behind us an elephantine snarl rose, fell and then rose again as we went through the gears. I was frightened and excited. A new physical pain shot through me, at once hurting me and giving me pleasure. The force of the wind wrapped my hair round my face and then whipped it back and then scrambled it away again, so that half the time I was seeing the road, the verges and the hedgerows through a black tangled veil.

Once we narrowly missed an army truck and once a farm wagon – drawn, incredible as it now seems, by two horses. The driver shook his fist at us and Bill Ogilvy grinned.

If anyone had been there to have told me that only an hour before I had been walking dreamily through the calm of a bluebell wood I should have called him crazy or a liar.

We climbed a hill. Beech woods hid the sky and occasional big creamy balloons of hawthorn blossom went flying past like driven clouds. The noise of Chloe's exhaust, louder than ever now, was a siren of exhilaration that finally stopped like the burst of a bomb, setting up a frightened cackle of jackdaws from the emerald skein of beech-leaves overhead.

I lay back for some time and gazed up at these beech leaves. They looked almost transparent in their fresh young tenderness. The oasis of which they were part was now as unreal as the bluebell wood of an hour before and I could only lie and gaze at them in stunned disbelief, wondering what sort of planetary excursion had brought me there.

A few minutes later Bill Ogilvy called me Liz and, with a gravity I'd never expected in him, kissed me. Nobody had ever called me Liz before; nor, incredible as it also seems, had anyone ever kissed me.

I lay there in a strange vacuum. I couldn't believe anything of what happened. I heard a blackbird scream down the road, clearly frightened by something. A remotely distant sound of planes humming across the sky like bees gradually grew louder and louder and finally screamed over us, not more than a quarter of a mile away.

'Spits,' Bill said. 'Coming home to tea.'

I shut my eyes and let the sound of the Spitfires die away; then I opened my eyes and stared up at him and said in a whisper:

'Do you know what you just did to me?'

'Incredible as it may seem, I believe I do.'

I slowly held up my lips and then, again with that altogether unexpected gravity, he kissed me for the second time. It was a moment quite rapturous enough in itself but he crowned it by a remark that suddenly had me caught, in exquisite suspense, between laughing and crying.

'I think I like you even more than my Chloe,' he said. 'Again? Once more? Wizard girl. Good show.'

And there was I, gaily flying upside-down.

3

YES: it was a good show. Everything, slightly ridiculous though it may now sound, was absolutely wizard. What was more I wanted it to last for ever and was quite sure, in my very young heart, that it would .

Two days later we scrambled. Ordinarily, of course, I should have said we moved – my grandmother, Harry and I – into the bailiff's house. This was a former dower house in almost orange brick standing a quarter of a mile beyond the other side of the lake, with a small pretty garden and a fine dove-cot, in that same lovely shade of brick, with a white weather-vane and a big magnolia growing up the side. I mention this magnolia because later that summer, when it flowered in August with its huge creamy chalices of blossom that might well have been carved from marble, it had ceased, for me, merely to be a tree in flower; but I will tell more about that later.

Meanwhile my mother moved to Malvern where, as I said to my grandmother with gay laughter, I hoped the waters would comfort her. I laughed a good deal in those first days of up-heaval, often without really being aware of it, and my grand-mother noted it shrewdly. She for her part had no cause for laughter; nor had Harry, who blundered about like a big lost sheep dog unable, after years of living in a big house, to find his bearings in a little one.

By contrast I found the smaller house delightful. I felt in-finitely more free in it than I had ever felt in the older, far larger one. The feeling of being imprisoned by walls and black-outs and snow and sheer size left me completely. My great happi-ness didn't arise, of course, simply from this. It stemmed directly from Bill Ogilvy, the beloved and fantastic Chloe and those even more fantastic moustaches. It was nurtured by the new and wizard language I had to speak. It thrived because everything was wizard. The weather was wizard, as it was to be all summer. The mad drives in Chloe up to the big beech woods on the hills were wizard. The hours Bill and I spent drinking shandy in small secluded pubs were wizard. The laughter and the utter foolishness of our talk was wizard. To be kissed by Bill with that curious combination of gaiety and gravity was wizard. Above all the very fact of being young and alive and loved was the wizardest thing of all.

I really believe I also thought the war was wizard, even though in a sense it still hadn't begun. That strange sense of unreality still hung over southern England. It was impossible to believe that that lovely pastoral landscape of ours was under any sort of shadow. Every day, it's true, we heard the growl of distant artillery fire; every morning, as regularly as a milkman calling, the Luftwaffe made its reconnaissance flights, though I was blissfully unaware of it at the time. Air raid sirens screamed and all clears sounded. Planes buzzed about the sky, sometimes at great heights, often invisible, like hornets. Bill frequently flew sorties, at the same time countenancing me with considerable seriousness not to ask about them. My grandmother knitted considerable numbers of long white hospital socks and Harry growled for hours beside the radio, again like a dog suspicious of every sound, grumbling that authority never told you anything and what a way it was to run a war.

But the greatest piece of unreality was the big empty house. Having been thrown out of it in little more than forty-eight hours we waited expectantly for the new merchant adventurers, as my grandmother sometimes rather acidly called them, to move in. Nothing happened. Almost every day I walked over to look at it. I peered in at the windows, looking at the boxed-in staircase, the carpetless floors, the billiard table shrouded in sheets. Dust had started to gather everywhere. Big dead blowflies lay about the window sills. Cob-webs were beginning to skein themselves about the cornices. Sheets of old newspaper lay about, growing yellower every time I looked at them.

At first I felt keenly about this. I thought it to be, as my grandmother did, callous and inhuman and really cruel. Then I got it off my chest by asking Bill about it. He said it was just the way it was. Nobody ever blasted well knew what was going on. He supposed some dim chair-borne clot of a type at Air

Ministry had forgotten to pull his finger out. There was too much frigging about and bumf and so on to get things done. You never got the gen.

Apart from this I was really very good about not asking about things. My seclusion had been such that I then had only the very vaguest idea where the nearest air-field was; it was, in fact, four miles down the railway line. When Bill spoke of Ops. and scrambles and Maggies and Mae Wests and gen and Brown Jobs and flaps and gremlins and kites and so on I was thrilled by the new syntax but innocently unaware of what most of it meant half the time. My needs and their accompanying ecstasies were really, in a sense, very simple. I didn't want to know too much. There wasn't any need for too many questions.

But one afternoon, as we lay on the hills, under the beeches, staring up at the expansive fragmentary pattern of blue and emerald, I did ask a question. Out in the distance I could hear a solitary plane coming in from the direction of the coast and something suddenly made me say :

'If that was a German plane would you know ?'

'My dear Liz !'

'But would you really ? I mean what sort ?'

'They'd throw me out on my 'ear-'ole tomorrow if I didn't.'

'What sort of plane is that one ?'

'A Maggie.'

'Do you fly Maggies ?'

'Little girls mustn't ask questions.'

'Where do you suppose it's coming from ? France ?'

'Hardly.'

The question I really wanted to ask had still to come and in my innocence I now asked it.

'Will you ever have to go away ?'

'You're just a load of offal when it comes to posting. Just a bod.'

'I mean would you ever have to go to France for instance ?'

'Might.'

'Nothing much seems to be happening over there, does it ?'

'Not much.'

'Would you like to go to France ?'

'Like Hell I would !'

He said this with enormous vehemence, like a boy being offered a vast plum cake, and I felt a great chill go through my heart. The shadow of a terrible thought also crossed my mind and for a time I lay absolutely quiet, without a word.

'Something the matter?' he said.

'No.'

'You're very quiet all of a sudden.'

'Am I?'

'France,' he said. There was tremendous relish in his voice. 'Champagne three and six a bottle. Wizard.'

I lay very quiet again.

Perhaps this makes clearer what I mean by asking too many questions. It was asking questions that brought me face to face, that afternoon, with the first of many substantial realities. The trouble was that I wasn't ready, in my innocence, to face them in return. Instead I simply asked another question and a pretty silly one it was.

'Do you really love me?'

'My mother once overheard a woman ask the same question and her man said "You know cuss well I do".'

He laughed and leaned over and kissed me.

'You're very sweet,' I said.

'You too. You too.'

'Flatterer. That's all you are. Just a big, big flatterer.'

'Wounding words. Very wounding words.'

'I don't think you could be truly serious if you'd tried for a month of Sundays.'

'Try me.'

'If you did by any chance go to France would you love me just the same when you came back?'

'I'd bring you oceans of champagne and Chanel and Camembert and silk panties and all things nice.'

'I can't wait for the day,' I said and lay very quiet again.

Just before we walked out of the wood to walk to the road, where Chloe was parked, I did another foolish thing. As if I hadn't already asked enough questions that afternoon I now asked yet another. Something made me say:

'Do you know a boy named Tony Johnson? A pilot. He comes from here. He's in France. Flying Spits, I think.'

33

'Not in France.' If it was a careless word it was almost the only one I ever heard him utter. 'Because there ain't none there.'

'Well, he's over there anyway. Flying something.'

In reply he looked up at the sky, lost in a remarkable rapture of his own.

'Lucky bastard,' he said, 'lucky bastard.'

When I got home, half an hour later, there were cucumber sandwiches for tea. The mention of cucumbers may sound slightly ridiculous too but it is also significant. Authority, in its magnanimity, had allowed us to keep our glasshouses, so that to the long string of useless slogans urging us along the path of war, such as *Digging for Victory* and *Lend to Defend Whatever It Was*, we were able to add our own, which might well have been *Peace Through Cucumbers*. But this wasn't all. I read somewhere, much later, that when you eat cucumbers there is a taste of Spring in your mouth. But the taste of Spring isn't always sweet, and the taste I felt in my mouth that day was a cool, sharp one.

I had made a rapid drop, in fact, from extreme exhilaration to chilling doubt, and my grandmother wasn't slow to notice it. In her wisdom and shrewdness she hadn't asked much about my absences from the house, some of them long and late, but now she said.

'Lately you've been so gay. Now you're surprisingly quiet all of a sudden.'

'Am I?'

'You're not by any chance in love, are you?'

'As a matter of fact I am.'

'I suspected it.'

'You sound as if you disapprove.'

'On the contrary.'

'You actually mean –'

'I think it's high time,' she said.

Considering that these were the first words we had exchanged on the subject it was uncommonly acute of her to detect a change in me that day. But that was typical of her and she went on :

'May I know who he is?'

I told her. 'Perhaps you remember him from that morning when the officers came to take over the house.'

'Ah! yes. The one with the very large moustaches? By the way has he any explanation as to why they still haven't moved in?'

I said he hadn't. He could only suppose that some clot of an Air Ministry type had forgotten to pull his finger out.

'What an extraordinary expression. What on earth does it mean?' she said and looked very hard at me.

I said it was just a figure of speech and helped myself to another cucumber sandwich.

At this point Uncle Harry came exploding into the sitting-room, which was hardly large enough to accommodate my grandmother and me with ease, let alone Harry, who had just been to the village to buy an evening paper, which he now struck loudly with the flat of his hand as if he were slapping a recalcitrant horse.

'Nothing in the damn thing as usual. I'm blessed if I know why I buy the wretched thing every evening. It merely repeats what you've already heard on the radio and then the radio repeats what you've read in the paper.'

My grandmother countered this remarkable piece of logic by saying 'I suppose you won't really believe the war has started until we all wake up one morning to find ourselves bombed in our beds. '

Heavily ironic, Harry said: 'Ah! but we won't. Our great Air Force friends will see to that. The great takers-over of other people's property. What a farce.'

'There's no need to throw insults about,' I said, 'even if it is.'

'Ah! so we're on our high horse, are we? We're on our high horse.'

'Yes, we are,' I said and glared at him with what I hoped was some of my grandmother's own imperious scorn.

With that he struck the back of a chair with great fierceness with his paper and stalked out.

'He does lose his temper so,' I said. 'He does bang about.'

'You were not exactly sweet-tempered yourself.'

'Oh! there's nothing wrong with me.'

She made no comment on this. She knew perfectly well there was. I was irritable, uncertain of myself and wanted someone to quarrel with. I was in consequence aggrieved that Harry should have walked out and taken the opportunity away from me.

A few minutes later I walked out myself. It was a very beautiful evening, full of a high sea-washed light, and in a field down the road some farm hands, helped by two soldiers in khaki shirts and trousers, were tossing rows of hay with pitch-forks. The evening air was delicious with the fragrance of hay but my mood was dark and when one of the soldiers whistled at me as I passed I tossed my head in great indignation and strode scornfully on.

Greater experience would have told me that evening that I wasn't in love, but the experience wasn't there. I was bold with the conviction that I was in love and nagged by a doubt that I wasn't really loved in return. In this mood I started to quarrel with myself as I walked along, occasionally breaking off to quarrel with a too persistent cuckoo whose mocking, aggravating voice was hardly ever quiet across the fields.

In this way I walked across to Hudson's land and finally saw Tom and his father and two oldish farm-hands making hay too in one of the smaller meadows by the river. Everything was very early that year and farmers were trying to wrest as much from the land as quickly as they could.

The four men had just knocked off for tea and were sitting with their backs against a hay-cock in the centre of the field. I sat for a time on a gate and watched them before Tom at last happened to turn his head and saw me sitting there. At that he put down his tea mug and brushed his hand across his mouth and walked across the field to talk to me.

'Hullo,' he said. 'Haven't seen you for donkey's years.'

That expression irritated me too and I merely said 'No?' rather archly.

'Well, I say I haven't seen you —'

'Make up your mind.'

'I meant I'd seen you quite a few times from a distance but not to talk to.'

'Oh! really.'

The pastoral scene of the hay-field in the evening sun mocked my ridiculous mood just as surely as it mocked the notion that war was a reality about to burst on us.

'Quite a smart little job, that sports car.'

'Yes, it is rather wizard, isn't it?'

'I see you speak the language.'

'Yes.'

'I hear them quite a lot of an evening. Down in the pub. Quite a gay lot. I've seen your friend with the moustaches there a time or two. He seems to be the gayest of the lot.'

'Bang on.'

'Have you seen him stand on his head and down a pint? That wants a bit of doing.'

'Things like that are a piece of cake to Bill.'

We went on talking in this fashion for another minute or two before he said he thought he ought to be getting back and then added, almost as a casual after-thought :

'They've moved into the house, I see.'

'They've *what*?'

'Been moving since crack of dawn.'

'I don't believe it.'

'I had to go down to the forge about nine o'clock to have a repair done on a coupling and they were moving in then. Truck loads of stuff.'

'All I can say is you're better informed than we are.'

'I went down and picked the coupling up about an hour ago and it looked as if they were really in. The place actually looked civilized.'

'Well, thanks for telling me. It's nice to know.'

The coolness of that last remark, like the rest of the conversation, must have given him some pain but I was too obtuse, too wrapped up in my own private vexations, to notice it. Grieved and irritated as I was by the suspicion that Bill might not be in love with me it never once remotely occurred to me that Tom Hudson might have been in love with me instead.

Tangling in fresh irritations, I walked slowly home, feeling like a child turned out in the cold. You might have thought, I told myself, that the business of moving into the house was some monstrously important official secret that couldn't be divulged for fear of betraying the country. It was security gone mad and I felt as if I had been soundly wounded and betrayed myself.

'Bill,' I told myself, 'I hate you. I hate you. I really hate you,' and finally dragged myself to bed and inconsolably wept myself to sleep.

Only three days later my grandmother opened an envelope at the breakfast table, took a card from it, peered at it for some moments with keen black eyes and then said:

'Well, I must say the Air Force moves fast when it does move.'

'That's the nature of the beasts. What is it now?'

She read from the card: 'Group-Captain L. T. P. O'Brien, A.F.C., O.B.E., D.F.C., requests the pleasure of the company of Mrs Catherine Cartwright and Miss Elizabeth Cartwright to the Officers' Mess, Bracehurst, on May 2nd. Cocktails 7–9 p.m.'

I suddenly felt very excited.

'Wizard. Will you go?'

'Of course I shall go. You know I adore parties.'

'May I have a new dress?'

'You had one for your birthday.'

'Oh! let me have another. A ravishing new one, please.'

'We'll see.'

'Oh! I wonder what sort of party it will be,' I said. I wrapped my arms about myself in excited anticipation. 'I wonder what sort of a party it will be.'

'I wonder.'

And we may well have wondered too.

4

I WENT to that party with two intentions firmly fixed in my mind : to look, in the first place, as ravishing as possible and to be as cool as was humanly possible to those too handsome barley moustaches. My intention, in fact, was to wither them. I inherit a great deal of pride from my grandmother and for three days I had kept myself apart, self-pitiful, angry, aloof, stubborn, and thoroughly wretched. I hadn't even answered a hastily scribbled note from Bill which simply said : 'Busy as a bee. But not too busy to see my lovely Liz. Meet you at *The Olive Branch* at 8 tonight.' Olive Branch, my foot ! I thought and didn't turn up.

In the matter of beauty I succeeded, I thought, rather wonderfully. My new dress, sleeveless and cut rather low at the neck, was of a curious and haunting shade of green, a sort of smoky Chinese jade colour. My skin is very slightly sallow and my eyes and hair, like my grandmother's, are very dark. For about a year my figure has been losing its puppiness and was now everywhere as firm as an apple. My breasts were neither too large nor too small and were moulded so well that I even scorned support for them.

The party began, as parties are sometimes apt to do, rather decorously. Our big drawing-room had been transformed into the mess ante-room, with a bar at one end and various squadrons' coats-of-arms adorning the walls, together with coloured pictures of Hurricanes and Spitfires and Gloster Gladiators. A big shining wooden propeller hung over the bar and a glistening silvery model of a Spitfire stood on a shelf underneath it, guarded by a positive palisade of bottles. The only hint of indecorum at that early stage was the sight of a dumpy and very pink *padre*, already pleasantly drunk, sucking at a quart silver tankard of beer as he leaned against the white napery of the bar-front, a sight at which no one but myself seemed in the least surprised.

When we entered the room Group-Captain O'Brien came

to greet us with what was almost old-world charm, shaking hands with us and bowing with much politeness.

'I hope you won't faint, Mrs Cartwright, at what we've done to your lovely old house,' he said.

'I am not,' my grandmother said, 'in the habit of fainting.'

The ante-room was full of blue uniforms and youthful faces. Large moustaches and young girls were scattered among them in about equal proportion but when the largest of the moustaches started to bear down on me like some swaying brown outrigger I contrived a sudden air of coolness and what I thought was distant hauteur. It simply wasn't any good. I needn't have bothered. My avowed intention of withering the Ogilvy emblem went for a heavy and immediate Burton.

'My dear old Liz. My sweet, long lost Liz.'

'Not so much of the old and not so much of the long lost.'

'My sweetest Popsie.'

'I am not your Popsie.'

'What will you drink? Sherry, gin, wallop, whisky, wine?' He grinned all over his face and I felt myself start grinning too. 'Punch? Admirable punch. *Specialité de la Maison*. Origin unknown. Monks or something. Pleasant and quite innocuous. Which will it be?'

I was about to say sherry when I changed my mind and said 'Punch.' A white-coated mess steward was passing and Bill stopped him and gave the order and said:

'Must introduce you to the chaps. Who's about? Ah! Splodge, old boy. Splodge – Miss Cartwright – our dearly beloved Liz, in whom we are well pleased. Liz – Pilot-Officer Miles Bannister, otherwise Splodge. Bad type.'

I shall never forget that first meeting with Splodge. Anything less like a bad type it would be hard to imagine. Splodge was modest, slight, soft-mannered, smooth-cheeked, very fair and almost heart-breakingly young. His wings were up but on the other hand it looked as if hair would never grow on his face at all.

'Good evening, Miss Cartwright,' he said in a treble voice so soft that it half gave me the impression that it hadn't even broken yet.

'Liz and her grandmother lived in the house,' Bill explained,

40

'until us shockers pinched it. Grandma tore us off a strip, I fear.'

'It must have broken your hearts,' Splodge said.

'My heart,' I said, in imitation of my grandmother, 'doesn't break so easily,' and the words, so casually thrown away, might well have been my own epitaph.

Curiously enough they seemed instantly to endear me to Splodge and it was he who took the glass of punch from the steward's silver salver when it came. The punch was a strange green shade and Splodge, as he handed it to me, was quick to notice that it almost matched my dress.

'What a beautiful combination,' he said and gazed with shy approval at my neck line.

'Beware of this type,' Bill said. 'Behind that innocent exterior lurk dark Satanic motives.'

'Cheers,' Splodge said and gave me the slightest of smiles as he raised his tankard of beer.

'Cheers,' I said.

'Cheers,' Bill said. 'Good show.'

Presently Bill left us. He was going to gather up more chaps, he said. Splodge and I half-looked at each other for fully a minute before I said:

'Funny man.'

'Hell of a good bloke.'

That cured a bit of my vanity and merely for want of something to say I said:

'What did you do before the war?'

'I didn't. I came practically straight from school.'

'What did you want to do?'

'Play the violin, actually.'

'Well, there's still time.'

'Is there?'

There wasn't time, though I didn't know it at that moment, and the question hung above us, unanswered.

'Do you like it here?' I said.

'Yes. I like the lake. I think the lake is very beautiful.'

'Soon the water-lilies will all be in bloom. It looks at its best then.'

I thought for a moment that he was going to say something

more about this but he merely looked past me with those heart-breakingly young, almost juvenile eyes, just as if he hadn't heard.

Bill, ever jovial, now came laughing back into our company, bringing with him a short wiry man a good ten years older than Splodge. His hair was thinning noticeably at the temples but it wasn't this that I noticed so much. What really struck me most about him was his immensely powerful wrists, almost out of proportion for so small a man.

'Flight-Lieutenant Burnett,' Bill said. 'Matters to you.'

'I sincerely hope it matters.'

A triple explosion of laughter almost blew down the chandelier in the ceiling above us as I said this.

'Good show, good show. Dear Liz. Damn good show.' Bill waved a jocular, approving tankard. 'Bless your splendid little heart.'

I begged that my heart should be left out of it and wanted to know, if possible, what black I'd put up now?

'Oh ! no black, Liz dear.'

'Then perhaps you might explain.'

'Mountaineering type.' Bill put his hand on the Flight-Lieutenant's shoulder with a sort of tender irony. 'Crazy man. Matters is merely short for Matterhorn, off which mountain he once fell when young.'

'Slanderous words. Duels have been fought for less.'

'He wakes i' the night and babbles o' South cols and crevasses.'

Once more we all exploded with laughter and again I thought the chandelier would come down. After this, without really knowing it, I drained my glass, whereupon the Flight-Lieutenant peered politely into it and asked if he might know what my poison was ?

'Oh ! yes – I see. Punch. Nice ?'

'Delicious.'

'Then I shall bring you another.'

'Good party,' Bill said. 'Going to be a good party,' and took a long exploratory glance round the now-crowded, babbling room and finally said, almost under his breath :

'Beautiful two-engine job over there, old boy.'

I wanted so much to be in the conversation and suddenly wanted to know which were the two-engine jobs? Spitfires?

Bill was instantly struck with a sobbing attack of apoplexy and leaned in a state of half-collapse on Splodge's shoulder, to be comforted there by a mock-tender hand.

'I cannot bear it. I cannot bear it. It's more than the jolly old frame can bear. Liz, my precious, please –'

The Flight-Lieutenant now came back with my glass of punch and, confronted by the sight of the helplessly muttering Bill, demanded to know :

'What? Already?'

'Tell him. Tell him, Splodge, old boy. He must be told.'

Feeling mildly foolish and bewildered I waited for Splodge to whisper in the Flight-Lieutenant's ear. Tears were running down Bill's cheeks, even as far as the moustaches, and I demanded to know at last what my latest black could be?

'Tell her, Matters old boy,' Bill said, 'As doyen of the party you must tell her. Tell her, please. Quickly. If 'twere done, 'twere well 'twere done quickly.'

The Flight-Lieutenant took me aside and whispered in my ear. I felt still more foolish as I listened but somehow, in those few moments, I also grew up a little. And finally I turned to them and said :

'May this little two-engine job rejoin the squadron now?'

'You're in!' they said. 'You're in!' and I felt that all of them could have kissed me.

This incident was hardly over before Bill was breaking out into mock protestation once more.

'Oh! no. Oh! no. Oh! no. Go away, go away! Cover her face, Splodge, she's too young. She mustn't be exposed to this. Not this, please. Not this.'

The officer who had now suddenly joined us was very tall. His long face was both bony and bone-coloured. The cheekbones were high and the jaw lean and oblong. The proud slate-grey eyes were somehow both pained and painfully handsome. His fingers were long and bony too and the left hand held in it a long amber-green cigarette holder.

'Go away!' they all said. 'Go away! This is England. Foreigners not admitted.'

'Good evening, gentlemen. I profoundly beg your respective pardons.'

'Not granted! Go away!'

'May I be introduced?' he said and with the most unflickering and penetrative eyes I had ever seen looked straight through me.

'This, unfortunately,' Bill said, 'is the Count. Count Dimitriov Mihail Sergei Zaluski. Miss Elizabeth Cartwright – the Count.'

He now gave me the most enchanting of smiles, bowed, and kissed my hand.

'Flannel!' they all said. 'Flannel!'

'I am most honoured, delighted and charmed to meet you, Miss Cartwright.'

'Flannel! Flannel!'

'You do not look typically English, Miss Cartwright, if I may say so.'

'Why? I am very English.'

'You look more as if you might come from my country.'

'And where is that?'

'Poland.'

'No: I am very English,' I said.

'Which is better. Much, much better.'

A great insincere and collective sigh went up from the other three officers. It was a very beautiful performance, they would have him know. A very beautiful performance.

'I am very glad to know I am appreciated.'

'Flannel! Flannel!'

'And if I may say so,' the Count said, 'beauty is not always in performances' and looked straight down at my partly bare bosom, so that I felt I had no dress on at all.

So we bantered our way through the first part of the evening. I am not sure now how many glasses of punch I drank or how many more officers I met but as the spring darkness came on I began to feel that innocuous green mixture roving its way inside me in twisting, simmering spirals. I began to feel very gay and from time to time, across the crowded room, I caught glimpses of my grandmother, very gay too, holding court with other officers. The laughter she aroused seemed to be even louder

44

than the laughter I aroused. There was, in fact, great laughter everywhere. We might have been celebrating the end and not the beginning of war.

As the late dusk came down the party was buzzing like an over-turned bee-hive. An occasional glass crashed to the floor. I lost all count of time. At irregular intervals the moustaches of Bill Ogilvy mysteriously disappeared and were just as mysteriously replaced by other moustaches. Once Bill returned and with a rush of overpowering sentimentality kissed me full on the lips and declared himself for ever to be true and promptly left me for the little two-engined job, blonde as oat-straw, in a tight black dress, sitting on a bar stool. This prompted two other officers I didn't know at all to kiss me too, but merely in passing, on the forehead. In turn this prompted the Count to run a light exploratory hand down my right thigh and ask if I wouldn't do him the great honour of having dinner with him the following night? I thanked him and said I had six invitations already and that I would try to sort out my diary the following morning, though in fact at that time I didn't keep one.

'I have never seen anything more beautiful,' he said and pinched the softer parts of my thigh and pressed his face against my ear. 'Never, never more beautiful.'

It must have been eleven o'clock or more when I realized that Bill and Matters were no longer with us and that there was a sudden wild shouting and cheering from outside the house, as from a game of football.

'Going to be fun and games,' Splodge said and grabbed me away from the aggrieved Count and bore me outside and along the terrace, where a crowd of twenty or more officers had gathered, some of them standing on the stone balustrade and all of them looking up at the front façade of the house.

I looked up too. It still wasn't really dark and we could see what was happening by the light of a thin, faint moon. Bill had already climbed up to just beyond the first floor windows and Matters was close behind him. There seemed to be no kind of foothold on the wall except that from the window sills and I saw that Bill, to make things more difficult, was climbing it with a pint silver beer tankard balanced on his head. Matters had a pink enamel chamber-pot on his, worn like an air-raid warden's helmet. In strict mountaineering style the two officers were roped together.

'On to the south col !' a wag shouted.

The tankard on Bill's head swayed, quivered and almost fell. Bill waved a cheerful right hand, then steadied the tankard with an almost elegant hand, like a man with a topper.

'Is it full?' I asked, again in my innocence.

'Well, the tankard is,' Splodge said.

Slowly Bill drew himself up by his finger tips, groping up the wall. Above him the sky was full of stars and once or twice I could have sworn that some of them were dancing on the chimney pots. At every inch of Bill's progress the tankard quivered and swayed and there were many hoots and much laughter from the terrace below. Every few moments my heart came into my mouth and once I groped too, feeling for Splodge's arm as my head went round.

All the time I knew that the tankard must fall but that Bill never would. If it isn't too ridiculous a word to use of that slightly mad situation of horse-play, laughter, chamber pots and stars I will say that I carried a conviction in my heart that Bill was immortal. If he fell from the wall he would simply bounce. But I knew quite confidently and simply that he would never die.

Finally the tankard did fall. First it swayed this way and that and then gave a slow totter. Bill moved with acrobatic desperation to save it but it pitched away, struck his right shoulder, hit the chamber pot with a loud donk ! and then drenched Matters in a fountain of beer below.

Officers everywhere fell about themselves in chronic disorder. Some groaned because they couldn't laugh. Others wept because they couldn't laugh any longer. One young pilot officer actually fell off the balustrade and into the rose-bud below, sereing the air with loud blue oaths. From the lake came a sudden splash as if someone had fallen into that too but hardly anyone took any notice of an incident of such triviality.

Matters' reaction to the fall of the beer tankard was merely to look casually up, as if the business of being struck by strange falling objects on mountainsides was an everyday occurrence, and then replace the chamber pot more firmly on his head. His hands were steady as steel and he moved slowly upwards with what seemed cool indifference, as if by means of steps cut into the brick-work.

'Excuse me, madam. Been looking for you everywhere. Compliments of Flying-Officer Devlin, miss.'

A mess orderly in white jacket stood by my side, holding a salver with two glasses on it. I hadn't the faintest idea who Flying-Officer Devlin was. It might have been that he was one of the officers who had kissed me casually in passing. It didn't really matter in that crazy moment and I simply picked up another glass of punch and Splodge picked up another glass of beer.

'Cheers,' we said to each other. 'Good show.'

To a great concert of cheering Bill reached the level of the stone cornice above the third floor window. In a moment of half-hysterical excitement I suddenly shouted 'That was my nursery up there! That window! My nursery!' and a young officer turned and gave me a stare of such blank astonishment that I might have been a baby crying in the night.

On the cornice Bill momentarily lost a footing. A lump of stone as big as a cricket ball broke off and struck the chamber-pot with yet another hollow donk! below. Unmoved, Matters continued to climb up, holding on, as it seemed, to nothing at all.

Finally Bill pulled himself up the last foot or so to the cornice and then sat there, brushing a casual hand across those vast moustaches in acknowledgement to the cheering gallery below. The fact of his having climbed to the very edge of my nursery window once again excited me absurdly and I danced up and down, cheering like mad. The stars danced too and in a ridiculous flush of hero-worshipping hysteria I was suddenly immensely proud of Bill and longed to be with him there, in the dizzy, starry heights.

Then Bill pulled Matters up the last foot or so by the rope and they both sat there on the cornice, grinning and waving. Then Matters took the rope off and started to lower it down the wall.

At this moment a very young, very dripping, very unsteady figure groped past me, muttering, not to anyone in particular but merely to the night air :

'Thought the bloody thing was concrete. Thought I was on the bloody apron. Bloody good show.'

Solitary in rumination he disappeared, dripping lake water, into the night.

I looked up to see two quart bottles of beer being slowly hauled heaven-wards by rope. When Matters and Bill had finally pulled them up the two officers stood smartly to attention, raised the bottles and drank.

'One, pause, two !' a wit shouted and a momentary tremor ran through Bill as he tilted the bottle.

'God,' a voice said, 'shakes me to the tits.'

'Good show !' we shouted. There was much raising of glasses and tankards. 'Good show !'

My innocuous glass was empty, but it was too late to wonder how and when I had emptied it. Suddenly the terrace, the house, the officers and the stars above the chimney pots started to go round and round me in a spiral I couldn't stop. For a moment Bill was no longer on the cornice and then suddenly was there again, amazingly duplicated. Then Matters disappeared and came back again and there were two of him too.

'Easy,' a voice said, 'easy,' and I found myself leaning unsteadily on the balustrade. A thousand officers were suddenly milling about the terrace but Bill and Matters and the Count were nowhere among them. I groped wildly and caught a uniformed arm.

'Bill,' I said. I wanted Bill to be with me very much. 'Oh ! there you are.'

'It isn't Bill.'

'No ?'

'It's Splodge.'

'Oh ! Splodge – Splodge, dear –'

I was vaguely aware of being taken by Splodge to the lakeside. I was even more vaguely aware of lying on the lake-side, on cool damp grass, and of Splodge holding my hand as I tried desperately to halt the rampant spiral of the stars in their courses. How long I was there I shall never know but later, I think long,

long later, I heard the sound of singing and I still remember the song :

> *Isn't it a Pity*
> *She's only got one Titty*
> *To Feed the Baby on —*

And at long last, to the far echo of that sad ballad someone — it might have been Bill or Matters or Splodge or Uncle Harry or all four of them for all I know — carried me away and gently put me to bed in the summer dawn.

5

IF that was the strangest dawn of my life up to that time an even stranger one, and far more important, was to begin some two weeks later. The party and the gay time were over; that morning the reality, or at least some part of it, began.

As I walked across the garden after breakfast there was nothing to show that that morning was any different from any of the many exquisite ones that presently were to make up that long summer. It was to be one of those summers when nearly every day is pellucid, when the weather is never too hot and when the bloom on the ripening wheat becomes an almost burnished golden-brown and is never tarnished by rain.

That morning many of the first roses, the blood red *Etoile d'Hollande* and that old pink variety *Caroline Testout*, were in bloom on the house wall. A tree of white lilac was in full blossom under the walls of the dove-cot. The sky was pure and very blue. There was hardly a breath of wind to swing the weathercock on the dove-cot roof and if the roof had been crowded with white doves – and by that time we no longer kept any – the scene could hardly have been more peaceful in its pastoral calm.

I lingered about the garden for perhaps ten minutes or so, thinking of Bill and wondering if I would see him that day. We hadn't met except for a brief lemonade at *The Olive Branch* since the night of the party. It once or twice occurred to me that he might just possibly have deserted me for the little blonde two-engined job and there were days when I felt angry and jealous because of it. But most of all I missed the particular brand of exhilaration he gave.

I had just decided to turn and go back into the house when I caught sight of Uncle Harry striding across the paddock that lay in front of the house. He was carrying a thick red-brown thorn stick and now and then, in his usual blundering fashion, he took savage swings at the heads of moon-daisies, cutting them off as clean as with a knife.

'You've heard the news, I suppose?' he said. 'We're going to lose an army. A whole damned army.'

So much had I been shut away in my own crazy private world that I had only the very vaguest idea of what he was driving at.

'See that?' he said. 'Can't you smell it?'

The only answer to this doubly contradictory question, which struck me as quite nonsensical, was to stand and stare.

'Over there!' He pointed savagely eastward, towards the climbing sun. 'Down towards the coast there. It's been thickening up for the last half hour or more.'

'Oh! I see what you mean. It's clouding over already.'

'Clouding over my Aunt Fanny. Look at it. Smell.'

The cloud that I now saw had gathered all along the eastward horizon, well below the sun, suddenly struck me as being very curious. It wasn't an ordinary cloud. In colour it was somewhere between snuff-colour and grey and it occurred to me that it might have been a sea-mist drifting in. We get that sort of sea-mist on this coast sometimes and when it blows in there's a sharp chill in the air.

'You know what that is?' He slammed the little wicket gate leading into the garden with such force that a rusty nail actually dropped out of it. He picked it up, swore and threw it into the field. 'You know what? I'll give you a thousand to one that's oil. Burning oil?'

'Burning where, do you suppose?'

'France. You weren't up early enough to hear the news bulletin.' There was a note of aggrieved shame, as well as anger, in his voice. 'We're going to lose an army. A whole damned army. Those poor blighters are being pushed into the sea. They've asked for every craft, yachts, paddle-steamers and God knows what, to go over there and take 'em off. God, what a shambles, what a God-awful shambles.'

I stood sniffing burning oil, having no idea what to say, and watching the slow uprising of that strange brown-grey cloud towards the region of the sun.

Suddenly he turned on me as if I were directly responsible for the defections of strategy that were now about to be visited upon us.

'I'll tell you something, young lady,' he almost shouted at

51

me. 'I'll tell you something. The damned Frogs have let us down. They've shopped us, my girl, lock, stock and barrel. I said they would. They live too well. They think too much about women and wine and their damn bellies.'

Before I could speak again I caught the sound of a squadron of fighters going over, pretty high up, and he heard it too.

'Your friends,' he said. 'What are they mucking about up there for? Why aren't they damn well over the other side in France, helping our chaps? That's where they're needed, aren't they?'

I said that perhaps it might be that some were needed in England too.

'Oh? Why? Why? Tell me why. If we lose the damn thing over there we've lost it here, I tell you. That's as sure as eggs.'

I opened my mouth to speak, but he shot me down, all guns firing.

'You know what will happen next? That other bastard'll be here. Invading us. After the Frogs, the Huns. God, what a shambles. What a God-awful shambles. It makes you sick.'

For the first time I started to feel a little sick too. The upper edges of that curious cloud, a few moments later, rose to the sun and there was a strange feeling of an approaching total eclipse in the air.

Harry stumped indoors and I followed him. In the sitting-room my grandmother was sitting by the window, knitting long white socks with her customary imperturbable calm. Harry strode up to the radio set, switched it on and, when it yielded no sound after a mere second or two, struck it a savage blow with his fist, almost as if to say 'That'll damn well teach you to answer when I speak to you!'

Presently popular music came forth and Harry snarled.

'That's all you ever get!' he said. 'Music. Damn cater-wauling.'

'Is something troubling you, Harry?' my grandmother said.

'We're losing an army!' he shouted. 'And I'll tell you something else. If we don't damn well watch out we'll lose the war.'

'Really.'

'Look over there.' He strode to the window and pointed eastward, where that strange cloud seemed at last about to eclipse the sun. 'See that? I've been watching it for an hour.'

My grandmother looked at the cloud and said, rather as I had done, that it was a pity the day was clouding over so early.

'Clouding over, my foot! That's oil. You can smell it. Burning on the French beaches.'

'I suppose that's possible.'

'Possible, possible? – it *is*. And you know what that means don't you? Invasion. I'll lay you a thousand to one we'll be invaded. Sure as eggs. Sure as tomorrow's Thursday.'

'It happens to be Friday.'

'Well, whatever it is! It's a damn job to know what day it is any day nowadays.'

None of this conversation had any visible effect on my grandmother's calm. Indeed as she took one further glance at the cloud which by now had completely eclipsed the sun she looked positively complacent.

'Why don't you go fishing or something?' she said.

'Fishing? My God. At a time like this? I tell you what, though.' Suddenly Harry jerked to a pause and a second or two later we were aware that a great brain-wave had gone through him. 'I tell you what –'

'Well?'

'I'll get my guns cleaned. At least I can get them ready.'

'You feel they would be of much use?'

'You never know,' Harry said. 'You never damn well know,' and suddenly made an almost triumphal departure.

For the next ten minutes or so I mooched about the house, half lost, not knowing what to do with myself. In my typically English fashion I didn't want to show my feelings but my sympathies were rather with Harry. Many emotions were bubbling about inside me and one of them, if I'd been honest enough to admit it, was fear; but the worst of them was uncertainty and I was both relieved and delighted when suddenly the telephone rang.

I rushed to it in the hope that it might be Bill on the line. Instead a piercing soprano demanded 'Are you all right, darling? It's me.'

It was my mother.

'Are you quite sure you're all right, Elizabeth darling? I dreamed you'd been bombed. It was all horribly clear. They were carrying bodies out of the house on a gate. They laid you out in the church. You and grandmother and Edna. It was really real, not like a dream at all. Are you quite, quite sure you're all right?'

'Absolutely. Everything's perfectly all right.'

'You sound tense.'

'It's early, that's all. You know I don't rouse up very easily.'

'I'm worried for you. I think you should come to Malvern. You feel it's absolutely safe here. You don't know there's a war on.'

'Is that a good thing?'

'Well, it's comforting, it's comforting. At least you can sleep well.'

'I sleep splendidly.'

'Yes, but you must admit you're sort of in the front line, aren't you? I mean with all those air-fields and so on. I mean that's where it's going to be fought, isn't it?'

'Where what is going to be fought?'

'Well, I mean we'll have to fight somewhere, won't we?'

'I suppose we will.'

'Is Mother there? I feel I must try to persuade her to come down here. You seem so terribly far away. Oh! by the way – before you go – there's something. I'm thinking of becoming a Catholic.'

'Good gracious, why?'

'Well, one's got to do something, hasn't one? One's got to do something.'

This conversation with my mother had the effect of restoring all my calm. I even felt a little smug. To be in the front line – well, perhaps there was nothing wrong with that. Perhaps it was no bad thing for morale.

'Well, one's got to do something, hasn't one?' I said to my grandmother when she had finished on the telephone, 'one's got to do something,' and added that I supposed she had heard about my mother becoming a Catholic.

'Oh! yes. But she'll soon get over that. There was a time when she was going to become a Theosophist. Unfortunately she hadn't the vaguest idea what it meant. She simply thought it sounded rather nice.'

'Actually I meant the bit about one must do something,' I said. 'I feel terribly lost this morning. I feel I must do something.'

'In that case you can walk as far as the glasshouses and get more cucumbers.'

We both laughed at that; our persistent cucumbers were always something of a joke with us.

'I suppose we *will* get through this tiresome thing some day, somehow,' she said. 'Well, if we do we can always say it was the cucumbers.'

'Yes, I suppose in a way you could say they were sort of symbolic of something – you know, cool –

'Tut, tut. Now don't get pompous, dear.'

Thus dismissed, I started to walk to the glasshouses, going the longest way round, by what we called the back road, first by *The Olive Branch* and then down by the church, where my mother had seen me so vividly laid out in her dream, and back through our village street of three shops, two more pubs, *The Welcome Stranger* and *The Pomfret Arms*, a couple of dozen houses, a Baptist chapel and a horse trough. One of the shops was also the post office and outside it a horse was actually tethered to the front railings. We hadn't even a petrol pump in those days.

It might in fact have been any morning in any peaceful year except for one thing. The cloud of smoke-haze that had earlier darkened the sun had now shut out most of the sky completely. The effect, as in a total eclipse, was a strange and eerie one. The earlier morning had been full of bird song but now the birds had stopped singing, with the result that you felt you were walking in an uncanny haunting vacuum.

As I walked down the street two army trucks went through, full of soldiers, who all waved and whistled madly. This time I waved in reply, a gesture that positively convulsed them with joy. 'Tonight?' one actually yelled and I grinned and waved again in answer.

After buying stamps at the post office I stopped to speak to Charley Bailey at the forge, half in the hope that Tom Hudson might turn up too. Charley, who actually touched his cap to me, was heating a long iron bar in the fire and while waiting for it to hot up said he thought that things looked bad and what did Harry feel about it all?

I said Harry thought they looked bad too.

'Does he think we'll be invaded?'

'He's sure of it.'

'I'm blessed if I ain't with him at that.'

Suddenly a crackle of machine-gun fire split the air very high up, far above that pall of cloud. The effect was to send both of us foolishly running into the street, where we stood for some minutes staring up, also rather idiotically, since there was nothing to be seen. When a second and longer burst of fire cut across the sky – it was a thrilling and exciting sound rather than one of portent or alarm – Charley nodded his head with approval and said something about 'they were the boys.'

'Well, it's nice to know they've got *some* friends.'

'My youngest boy's in that outfit. Bombers, though. Rear gunner.' In the pride of the moment he suddenly forgot himself. 'Arse-end Charlie. Oh! sorry, miss.'

'It's all right. I know all the words.'

'I expect you do. I've seen you a time or two with that officer in that little yellow car.'

'Yes.'

'Might be him up there.'

'Could be.'

Suddenly, from a mile or two away, there was the most appalling crump: I couldn't tell whether it was a bomb or a plane bouncing and simply said:

'Shaky do.'

'Sounded near,' was all he said.

It sounded, to me, even nearer than that. It sounded dead in the centre of my heart. I knew it could have been Bill or Splodge or Matters or the Count or anybody else I knew and the fact that I knew equally well that it couldn't did nothing to lessen the tension of my fear.

Charley went back into the forge and I stood by the open door, watching him. I had the feeling for a moment that he was going to say something more about his son but instead he took up his pincers and gripped the red-hot bar with them and turned it slightly and then worked the bellows, so that the coals glowed white-blue with heat.

'Know what?' he said. 'I'd like to run this bar through that blasted Hitler. Slow.'

I hadn't time to say anything before I heard the snarl of a sports car coming up the street. I joyfully rushed out of the forge, knowing Chloe's voice, and sure enough there she was, coming like a bomb. I started waving frantically and in seconds, brakes wailing, she pulled up twenty yards beyond me.

'Bill!' I called. Then I saw that in the driving seat sat not Bill but Splodge.

'Splodge!' I said. 'Whatever on earth are you doing in Chloe? Bill — Heavens above, he'll cut your ears off.'

'Lent it to me for five minutes. I left my gas-mask at the Mess and had to go back for it. The Wing-Co. tore me off a terrible strip.'

'How's Bill? Where have you all been?'

'Oh! things. Busy.'

'Bill hasn't rung me up or anything.'

'We're all so busy we hardly get time to shave. Give you a lift? I've got to go.'

'No, thanks all the same. I'm walking. Give Bill my love. Tell him I'll give him the old one-two if I find he's been with that blonde job.'

'No fear of that.'

'Tell him to ring me.'

'Good-bye, Liz. Simply must dash.'

'Must you? Well, you can give him this for me.'

I bent down quickly and kissed him lightly on the cheek. He grinned and the painfully young eyes glowed.

'Wizard. Absolutely made my day.'

In another moment I was waving good-bye and Chloe was far up the street, splitting the air with her waspish snarl.

All through the rest of that day I was restless and troubled. I kept recalling the crackle of machine-gun fire. My constant fear that it might have been Bill up there was counteracted by the equally constant irritation that he might have abandoned me for the little blonde two-engined job. And every half an hour or so, just to make things worse, Harry would barge into the house, switch on the radio for news, bark at it when there was none and then repeat the fretting catechism that I had heard so often before :

'First Poland, then Norway, then Belgium, then Holland and now France, by God. What a sell-out. By God, do you realize we're on our confounded own ?'

About half past nine I could bear it no longer. I picked up the first book I could lay my hands on and was just about to say good night to my grandmother when Harry came in from the garden and said, with heavy innuendo :

'I suppose the yellow sports car out in the road wouldn't be waiting for anybody, would it ?'

I ran out of the house, down the garden path and into the road, where Chloe was waiting, only to be brought up sharp by a repetition of what had happened in the morning.

'Bill –'

Again it wasn't Bill in the driving seat, but Splodge.

'But Splodge – where on earth's Bill got to ? I haven't seen him for such ages. He's just abandoned me.'

At first he didn't answer. Suddenly a dark fear ran over me and I seemed to feel all my skin shrink and tighten and grow cold and deadly dry. My disembodied voice was cold and dry and shrunken too.

'You're not trying to –'

'Oh ! no. Good God, no. Actually he's been posted, that's all. Him and the whole ruddy squadron. Two days after that party. They had about two split seconds to pack their gear.'

I didn't know whether to weep or shout with joy. I was trembling all over and for some moments I couldn't say a word. And when at last I did manage to form a sentence it was rather an acid one.

'I think someone might at least have had the decency to tell me.'

'Terribly sorry, Liz. But thing's have hotted up like hell lately. Nobody's had a minute to spare.'

All my fears and misgivings suddenly came rushing back.

'Splodge, you're not trying to tell me Bill's been killed, are you ? Please, for God's sake, if he has –'

'Good God, no.' He actually laughed at me. 'You can't kill blokes like Bill. He's not the type.'

Though I hadn't very much to be happy about I laughed too. An image of Bill standing to attention, beer-bottle in hand, under my nursery window, on that evening of early summer madness, made me recall my fond notion that he was immortal and my faith was restored.

'I suppose you're right – but my nerves have been on edge all day. Ever since –'

'Ever since what?'

'Just before I met you this morning there was the most awful bang. Bursts of machine-gun fire and all that and I couldn't help wondering –'

Splodge didn't say anything. He just sat very still, staring over the car-wheel, at some far-off distance.

'Did anything happen this morning?' I said. 'Was someone killed?'

'Yes. I'm afraid so. Devlin.'

Devlin? I couldn't for the life of me think who Devlin was.

'Who's Devlin?'

'Well, he isn't now. But you remember him.'

'No.'

'The Irish type.'

I couldn't remember any Irish type either.

'At the party,' Splodge said. 'You and he had a bit of an argument. I think you misunderstood something he said about England. I think you had an idea he didn't like England or something and you said well, if he didn't like it why did he bother to come over and fight for it? or something like that.'

The incident, which until then I had utterly forgotten, now came back to me.

'He was terribly cut up about it. Thought he'd put up a terrible black. His fault and all that,' Splodge said. 'That's why he sent you that drink.'

'Drink?'

'That enormous punch. Must have been a treble. The one that put you out.'

'God, what a stupid fool I must have been. Getting into an argument like that.'

'Just one of those things.'

It was just one of those things. The young Devlin, whom I hardly knew, was dead. And his face, which I could barely remember, suddenly started haunting me far more than if I had known it well. I felt I owed him a deep apology and was full of nagging and wretched reproaches that it was too late to make it now.

'Talking about a drink,' Splodge said, 'could you use one?'

'I might use two. Or even three.'

'You sound depressed.'

'I am.'

'About Bill?'

'Not so much. It's hard to explain. I sort of feel I haven't any right to be here.'

I got into the car and we drove up to *The Olive Branch* without another word. Inside the pub, in the public bar, several soldiers were drinking beer and two R.A.F. sergeants were playing darts with a couple of young farm hands. Splodge and I walked through to the private bar and I knew the sergeants and the soldiers were staring after me.

'Cheers,' Splodge said.

'Cheers.'

Splodge had bought a whisky for himself and a shandy for me.

I bitterly wanted to cry into that shandy. It may sound slightly heavy now, but that evening I felt as if I were being deeply reproached by the dead. It isn't a pleasant thing to hate yourself and it's even less pleasant when you don't quite know why.

'Cheers,' Splodge said. 'You look as if the end of the world had come.'

'I could jump in the lake,' I said.

At this he put his arm gently on my shoulder and looked at me so earnestly with those painfully young eyes of his that it merely made things worse and I could have wept aloud.

'You'll get over it,' he said.

And presently I did get over it, enough at least to ask about Chloe.

'How,' I said, 'do you come to have Chloe?'

'Bill sold her to me for thirty quid. With strings.'

'Strings?'

'I've got to sell her back to him for twenty-five when he gets back to England.'

'So he's gone to France after all.'

'God-awful clot. I shouldn't have said that. You didn't hear me.'

'France,' I said. 'He's happy now.'

After that, in some curious way, I set Bill aside. We didn't talk of him any more and we didn't talk about Devlin either. The summer dusk came slowly and after a time Splodge got hungry and Mrs Croft, the landlady, made us a plate of corned beef sandwiches and brought a pot of mustard to go with them.

While Splodge was digging into the blue mustard pot and spreading mustard on to his first sandwich Mrs Croft, a pleasant, pale, elderly body who at no time looked either very well or strong, started asking after my family. Was it true my mother had gone away?

'Yes. She's at Malvern. She's been trying her best to get us to join her there.'

'And will you go?'

'Not on your life.'

'Funny,' she said. 'That's how I feel. Anybody who wants me out of here will have to cart me out on a pitchfork.'

It was this remark of Mrs Croft's that finally restored my self-confidence. Then as we were finishing the last of the sandwiches Splodge said:

'You wouldn't like to hear some music, I suppose?'

'Music? Where?'

'I've got my portable gramophone in the bus. I thought we might listen to a few records. That's if you'd like to.'

'I'd love it.'

We finished up the last of the drinks and the sandwiches and said 'Good night' to Mrs Croft and went out and got into Chloe. Just before he started up the engine Splodge asked me if there was anywhere I'd particularly like to go to and I said:

'Let's drive up to the Devil's Spoon. I'll tell you the way.'

From the Devil's Spoon, a big grassy hollow on the crest of the downs where in spring great numbers of cowslips grow, you can look out on a great wide quilt of orchards and woodland and little villages and cornfields and pastures to a point where the smoke stacks of ships are just visible on the line of sea. On days of westerly wind big cloud shadows come sweeping in across it and on spring days the cowslips are tossed about like silent golden bells. They say that Caesar's legions camped here. Chaucer's pilgrims skirted through the big beech-wood lower down the hill, the very beech-woods where Bill and I had sometimes sat and listened to the sound of incoming planes, but that night there were neither legions nor pilgrims, wind nor cowslips to disturb a silence so vast that it was exactly as if, as someone later remarked, an entire nation was holding its breath. It was all deathly, ominously still.

'Don't put on the music yet, Splodge. I'd just like to sit and listen to the night.'

'Sort of music of the spheres?'

'Something like that.'

We didn't, as it turned out, put on any records at all. We simply sat listening, as I said, to the night. The sky was perfectly clear and there were a great many stars. Almost the only sounds we heard were an occasional call from an owl, a clock striking quarters from a village down below and once the sound of a plane stooging away in the west.

We didn't talk much either. Splodge put an arm round my shoulder and I felt a great sense of tenderness in the air. With Bill there really hadn't been any tenderness. With him it had all been a marvellous game, a sort of emotional helter-skelter. Perhaps that was why, though I had been dismally sure that my heart would break if Bill were taken from me, alive or dead, it now showed no sign of any such disaster.

Presently Splodge brushed his mouth across my hair and then, without a word, drew my face towards him and kissed me. I don't know why but I got the strange impression that this was the result of a solemn promise given long, long ago. I suppose I am really trying to say that it had in it a feeling of great inevitability. If there is a pre-ordained pattern to life, and there are times when I'm not at all sure that there isn't, this was the most pre-ordained thing that had ever happened to me. I knew I had been born for that particular moment in time and I accepted it with wonder.

And also with calm and joy. Curiously enough I felt a good

deal older. I suppose I grew up quite a bit that day but one thing at least is certain: I didn't ask any questions. The moment and its blossoming were enough.

Splodge didn't ask any questions either but at last simply said, very quietly:

'I like it here.'

'We must come again.'

'Yes.'

'By July there will be wild strawberries.'

'Wild strawberries? I've never tasted one in my life.'

'You're going to this year.'

And with these words I felt, for some reason, that summer had really begun.

6

In France, by this time, the battle had raged forward to inevitable doom with a swiftness and ferocity that couldn't escape even a girl like me. By June 9th German Panzers had reached the lower reaches of the Seine and Oise; presently they were on the Marne and in another week, on the 16th, had reached Orleans and the Loire. Paris had fallen even before this, on the 14th, and a great gap opened southward, past Dijon and Besançon, almost to the Swiss frontier.

The effect of all this on my Uncle Harry was to spur him to a frenzy of tireless activity in an endeavour to turn our little house into an armed fortress. A great pile of yellow sand arrived, together with several hundred sand-bags, and for days Harry and the two remaining gardeners, Baxter and Lines, laboured strenuously to fill the sandbags and then pile them four or five feet high about such strategic places as the steps leading to the coal-cellar, the windows of the gun room, the still room and the larder. Baxter, fearful that none of us would be able to have an egg for breakfast or a pie for dinner, begged to be allowed to go to market to remedy this desperate state of affairs and did so, coming back with a cockerel and a dozen Rhode Island Reds, six Khaki Campbell ducks and two Belgian hares. The hares, a buck and a doe, were duly hutched and a few spare sandbags piled over and about them too. The Khaki Campbells ranged freely about the meadow. From somewhere Baxter got an old baker's van, housed the hens in it and surrounded it with wire-netting, which was partly sand-bagged too. The sun-flaked words *Geo. Oakley Family Baker Finest Bread and Cakes*, still visible on the side of the van, were a great and curious comfort to us all.

It was as if we were preparing for a long siege. This impression was further strengthened by the fact that Harry also deemed it necessary to turn the house into an armoury. Baxter and Lines were fitted up with 12 bores. Of Harry's two pairs of guns one pair was kept in the gunroom; another gun he kept by his bedside and sought to insist that my grandmother keep another one by hers.

She would hear of no such thing.

'And what do you propose that I should shoot at? Owls?'

Harry pointed out that it wasn't of owls that he was thinking of but of Nazi parachutists, who would surely be upon us, at the least expected moment, any time now.

'What would you do if one of them dropped in the garden, eh?'

'Give him a whisky-and-soda and telephone the police.'

'And be raped meanwhile.'

'I cannot conceive even remotely that a man dropping from several hundred feet by parachute in enemy territory would have uppermost in his mind any such thing as the pleasures of intercourse.'

'People do strange things,' Harry said darkly, 'under pressure.'

'I've little doubt they do. In which case you'd better keep one gun on one side of the bed and one on the other. Then you can fire on both flanks.'

'All right. But you'll be very sorry if you look out of your bedroom window one fine morning and see an armed Hun floating down.'

'We will meet that eventuality,' she said, 'when it comes.'

In the middle of these crises, one military and one domestic, another and smaller one occurred, seemingly quite trivial in itself but in reality of great importance to me.

At the big house we had kept eight servants: two cooks, two housemaids, a sort of secretary housekeeper and three gardeners. In addition there were the bailiff and two game-keepers, one of whom acted also as river-keeper, but since my grandmother was inclined to be impatient, if not actually contemptuous, in her dealings with men, these three came under Harry's jurisdiction rather than hers. Of these servants the two cooks, the housekeeper, one housemaid, one gardener and the two keepers had been dismissed for the duration. We now had only Edna, who washed, ironed, darned, cooked, swept, waited at table and still starched Harry's stiff collars after the fashion of 1910, and the two gardeners, who ran the gardens and glasshouses of the big house on a commercial plan, sending produce to shops and markets.

A few days after the fall of Paris, at which time a stunned nation was still holding its breath, Edna came into the sitting-room one afternoon to announce that Rose had called and would Mrs Cartwright be good enough to see her?

Rose was the elder of the two cooks and presently was shown in, harassed if not actually haggard, visibly quaking and, as it presently turned out, on the verge of tears. Rose, sixtyish and always rather fragile, had taken a post as cook in a boys' school and had now met disaster in the form of a storming headmaster who, temper much-frayed by events, had accused her of stealing sugar. Everybody's temper was in fact frayed by events and people were apt to take it out on each other in a variety of disloyal and petty ways.

The infamy of being accused of theft had been too much for Rose, to whom honour and loyalty were as fundamental as breath. We all loved her and indeed my mother and grandmother had openly shed tears at her departure.

'If only I could come and assist part-time, ma'am. At week-ends, say, or when you wanted to give a little dinner party or a luncheon party for some friends.'

'I don't think that would be a very good arrangement, Rose. It's much too haphazard.'

'Then perhaps I could come and live in again, ma'am. I would come for less wages than I had before.'

'It's very kind of you to offer, Rose.'

'It must be a lot of hard work for Edna.'

'Indeed it is a lot of hard work for Edna. But the truth is we just haven't a spare bedroom.'

'Oh! this awful war,' Rose said and promptly burst into tears, as if not having a spare bedroom were the worst evil of the lot.

While Rose was stemming her tears I stood at the window, staring at the garden, over which the June heat was quivering like a hovering dragonfly. The nights had been very hot that week and I now recalled coming downstairs the previous night, about midnight, unable to sleep, to get myself a drink of cold water, only to find Edna still ironing in the kitchen.

Edna had a great fear of being bombed in her bed and had taken to working late in order to avoid the terrors of sleeping. As a result she had started to look haggard too and dark and heavy-eyed.

'Edna was working till after midnight last night,' I said. 'It isn't good. We'll have her crack up on us. And then what?'

'I know it isn't,' my grandmother said. 'But short of slinging a hammock up in an apple tree we just haven't another bed.'

'Edna and me could sleep two in a bed,' Rose sobbed.

'I've just thought of something,' I said. 'I could sleep in the dove-cot. I could turn that upstairs floor into a room for myself. It would be fun. I should love it.'

'There's no electric light there.'

'What's wrong with candles?'

'Nothing, I suppose.'

'Then why don't I? It's the simplest thing. The easiest solution.'

'Won't you find it rather lonely at night?'

'If I do I'll borrow one of Harry's guns and fire distress signals every half hour.'

'Oh! Miss Elizabeth, I'll come and help you flit!' Rose said and promptly burst into another flood of tears.

So it came about that, in the very centre of that early summer's bewilderment, cynicism and humiliation, I was once again insulated – but now it was to be for the last time – against the raw-edge of war. Just as I suppose we all think of ourselves as immortal so in the same way I never really thought, up to that time, that war could do anything even of merely unpleasant consequence to me.

I was like a child with a new dolls' house. My dove-cot was my very own and as I carried curtains and chairs and rugs and tables and mattresses and candlesticks and so on up to it I felt sometimes quite giddy with excitement. Unaware of its effect of insulation – that was to come rather later – I felt instead almost a feeling of jealousy, of being defensively in possession, so much so that I even remarked at breakfast one day, half-seriously, half-mocking:

'Visitors to the dove-cot are requested to ring three times.'

'And ask for Charlie, I suppose,' Harry said.

'*Not,*' I said, 'very funny.'

I thought the moment a good one, however, in which to ask my grandmother a question and I said :

'Would you object if I sometimes had a few friends in? Even a little house-warming party?'

'We are not sending you to a nunnery.'

'Thank you.'

'No late night stuff, though,' Harry said. 'I need my beauty sleep. I know these fellers.'

'I wonder,' my grandmother said.

Meanwhile, across the Channel, in France, despair and capitulation were presently complete. Somewhere, and I still wasn't even aware enough to guess where, Bill was among the Hurricanes being shot down at the rate of two hundred and fifty in ten days or two in every daylight hour. Soon a Frenchman blessed with great clarity of vision was announcing that within three weeks England would have her neck wrung like a chicken. To be friends with us, according to a certain Pétain, was merely 'fusion with a corpse'. It would be better, someone else said, to be a Nazi province and in answer, at Churchill's behest, men of all creeds, ages and classes started to form themselves into a volunteer defence corps and at last my Uncle Harry, gas-mask, shot-gun and haversack at the ready, was really happy as he crawled about church-yards, hedge-rows, rick-yards and woodlands in deadly serious and clumsy manoeuvre through summer night-times.

One evening about this time I walked as far as *The Olive Branch* in the hope of seeing Splodge or Matters or the Count or perhaps even Tom Hudson with the idea of inviting them to my first party. The little bar with its dartboard, pots of old bulrushes on the shelves and out of date notices about slate clubs stuck about the walls was almost empty : empty, at any rate, of Air Force men. Two surprisingly young farmhands, drinking shandy, stood talking, of all things, about cricket ; the local road-man, whose left ear had been shot off in the first world war and who in consequence bore a kind of angry pink mouse-hole in that side of his head, sat in a corner alone, morosely contemplating a half empty tankard. Fragile Mrs

Croft, the landlady, stood behind the bar, polishing glasses and looked rather withdrawn as she called me 'Miss Elizabeth'.

It was some time before an army sergeant came in, together with a private and a corporal, and started a lot of beef about things across the Channel. 'Was we there? I'll say we was bleedin' there. And a few thousand other unlucky bastards too. Like sitting on a wasps' nest and no bleedin' swatters. Oh! yes we was there. And where was they? The old posh wallahs. The jolly old prang brigade. Them up there. Not a bleeder in sight. Not a blue-arsed fly.'

I stood as much of this as I could, with the corporal saying in garrulous agreement 'S'right, mate, S'right, mate, S'right,' until I could stand it no longer and at last said :

'And what kind of outfit are you supposed to be? Do you need nursemaids?'

The sergeant gave me a very sergeant-like look and then surveyed me slowly up and down as if I were some stale half-baked tart or something and finally said :

'And who are you supposed to be fighting with? And, if I might say so, for?'

'God only knows,' I said. 'And if He does, He hasn't told me.'

'You're dead right.'

'So many Brown Jobs,' I said.

With this, in a state of near fury, I swept out. Someone, the corporal I think, blew me a raspberry, but I made no sign of having heard. It was all typical of the confused, contagious, groping bitterness of the time.

I walked almost blindly down the road in the evening sunshine. I didn't then know about those Hurricanes dissolving in the heat of battle at the rate of two every daylight hour, or that Spitfires, which we were being rousingly exhorted to help make by surrendering our aluminium kettles, were too precious to replace them. In my divine young ignorance I had some sort of idea that not only did Spitfires reproduce themselves, like mysterious galaxies of stars, but that also, as in galaxies, there were limitless thousands of them to reproduce themselves.

It is always a bad thing to be bitter about something without knowing quite what you are being bitter about, and this was as true of the sergeant as it was of me. Thankfully I ran into Tom Hudson at the bottom of the hill and I had never been quite so glad to see that heavily bronzed, blue-eyed face of his.

'I've just come from your house,' he said. 'I brought you a half-chip of cherries.'

Pleased though I was to see him I was still only half there. The rest of me was still arguing bitterly with the sergeant and some of my caustic confusion must have shown in my face, because Tom said:

'Well, you might look pleased. I thought you were so passionately fond of cherries.'

'I'm awfully, awfully sorry, Tom. It's just that –' and I went on to tell him of the dust-up with the sergeant.

'Everybody's bitter and on edge,' he said. 'I had a devil of a flare-up with my father the other night. We've never quarrelled before.'

'I'm sorry I wasn't there when you called. Did my grandmother tell you about the dove-cot?'

'Dove-cot?'

I told him, in my excited fashion, about the dove-cot, adding: 'I'm glad I saw you because I'm planning a little housewarming party. Probably next Sunday. I want you to come. Just you and some of the Air Force boys. They're a wizard crowd.'

It was now his turn not to be there. He suddenly seemed, I thought, both withdrawn and embarrassed. Nor did he say anything for quite some moments and those intensely blue eyes of his, which in very bright light had sometimes the look of being quite incandescent, now had a curious dilation about them behind his spectacles, as if they really were weak after all.

'I don't think I can manage Sunday,' he said at last. 'I've promised to drive over to Stanhurst to fetch Aunt Midge. She's been living all on her own there. She's scared of what might happen now and she's coming to live with us.'

It was a poor excuse, I thought, and I suddenly felt vexed and hurt. I couldn't for the life of me think why I should be hurt by Tom Hudson, for whom I felt nothing but ordinary neighbourly friendliness, and I tried not to show it in my face. But long afterwards Tom confessed:

'I know I hurt you that night when I said I couldn't come to your party. I could see it in your face. I wanted to come no end. But I felt it was like barging into a club when I wasn't a member.'

But all he said as we stood there at the end of the village street was:

'The cherries are very early this year. We've cleared a lot of trees already. I've known years when they'd hardly started by now.'

'There would have to be a war in a summer like this.'

'I know. That's another thing that gets people down.'

How long we might have continued this desultory conversation I don't know but suddenly I heard Chloe's musical roar and there she was, snarling up the street, with Splodge's squashy blue cap cocked to one side of his head behind the wheel. If you know anything about the arrival of heroes within the drab confines of ordinary mortals you will know how frantically I waved my hand.

Splodge pulled up Chloe with several explosive bangs and when the last of them had settled down to a mere rattle I heard Tom Hudson say:

'Good-bye, Elizabeth. I must go now.'

'Oh! don't be silly, Tom. Of course you're not going.'

'I really must.'

'If you do I'll never speak to you again.'

After that peremptory threat he stayed and I introduced him to Splodge. Not the least of Splodge's constant and more endearing virtues was his infinite modesty but it almost seemed, that night, as if he might have been carrying some sort of blatant banner with him, so oddly embarrassed did Tom look. To say that he looked suddenly like a man carrying the burden of an enormous inferiority complex is too facile. The strange thing is that that look of acute embarrassment made him look positively aloof. I suppose he might have thought that Splodge, in uniform, wings up and all that, might have looked down on him. Whereas it was exactly the other way about. It was almost as if he was looking down on Splodge.

'Well, let's all three have a drink,' Splodge said, at last switching off Chloe and so creating an enormous silence.

'Thank you very much,' Tom said, 'but I really must go. I've got all the locking up to do.'

'Tom's a farmer,' I said. 'He's just taken a big basket of cherries to the house.'

'Wizard. I adore cherries. Nicest fruit of all.'

'I'll bring you some if you like,' Tom said. 'They're pretty good this year.'

'By jove, really? Wizard.'

'Where can I bring them?'

'Oh! to the Mess.'

'Oh! yes. Is one allowed in?'

'Allowed? It's our home, old boy.'

'All right. I'll be along tomorrow.'

It sounds like the most ordinary and simple of conversations but because of it I felt my latent affection for Tom Hudson stir very deeply inside myself, turn over and then go completely to sleep again, exactly like a warm kitten.

After that Splodge and I went into *The Pomfret Arms* for a drink. This is rather more of a hotel than a plain pub. Its lounge bar has red carpets and oak settles and its walls flash with brass, battle-axes and copper. It occasionally puts on luncheons for shooting parties and on Boxing Day the Hunt meets outside. It isn't quite the place where embittered army sergeants incite women to fervent protestation and I was both relieved and glad simply to be able to sit on one of the oak settles, by a window, and stare at the roses in the back garden and drink sherry.

But my relief didn't last long. I sensed – quite correctly, as it later turned out – that there was something on Splodge's mind that night, but what it was I couldn't tell and didn't probe to discover. Splodge in turn seemed to sense that I suspected this and we hadn't been sitting there more than three or four minutes before he said:

'How would you like a surprise?'

'Wizard. I always go for surprises.'

'I got you a little present.'

'But it isn't my birthday or anything.'

'It's just a little something.'

Then he put his hand in his tunic pocket. Things must have been in a rare state of boyish untidiness in there because out came a handkerchief, a cocktail stick, a box of matches, a small green leather box and, of all things, a rabbit's foot. I stared at this last object for some moments in infinite astonishment before Splodge, looking very like a small boy who has been caught smoking in bed or something of that sort, shoved it back into his tunic pocket again.

'A rabbit's foot,' I said. 'Is that the surprise?'

'Oh! no. Good Lord, no.'

'What have you got it for?'

'I sort of carry it about.'

'But why?'

'Oh! it's a sort of thing. You know.'

Tom Hudson's painfully acute embarrassment was a mere shadow of the torturous blank that I now saw on the face of Splodge and I didn't improve it by laughing briefly and saying:

'You're like a squirrel, hoarding things.'

'No,' he said. 'No. This is the present.'

He then put the little green box in my hand. If up to that moment I had always thought of him as heartbreakingly young I now experienced a passionately ridiculous moment when I wanted to take him in my arms and hold him against myself like a child.

'Do open it,' he said. 'Perhaps you won't like it. I don't know.'

I opened the box and inside was one of those old-fashioned Edwardian gold lockets on a thin gold chain. I remember thinking for a moment that it looked rather painfully provincial and then he said:

'Turn it over. Look on the back.'

'My initials. Did you have them put on?'

'They were already on. That's what made me buy it.'

I simply looked at him in silence. He stared back at me in painfully solemn and tender adoration, not speaking a word either. There is always a great pain about first love, especially in moments when there is no way of expressing it, and I felt my lips tremble and my throat tighten with an unbearable longing for him.

'Don't look at me like that,' he said at last. 'I can't bear it.'

'I can't bear it either.'

I gave a sort of half smile and bit my lips and he said :

'Do you like it?'

'The locket? Awfully.'

Then I could bear it no longer and looked quickly round the room and said in a half whisper :

'I want to kiss you very, very much but as I can hardly do it in the lounge of *The Pomfret Arms* will you please take me somewhere where I can?'

We drove up to the Devil's Spoon. We lay on the grass and looked up, during long silences, at the early stars. He kissed me over and over again and at last when he started to run his finger-tips over my breasts I did nothing to stop him. Finally he undid my dress and took out my breasts, one by one, and kissed them.

I wanted to cry with happiness. That was the first time I ever went to eternity. I was to go on a good many other occasions later but that night I went farther into the outer spaces of joy than I had ever been before or had remotely dreamed was possible.

We must have lain there till well past midnight and at last I said :

'You never really told me about your rabbit's foot.'

'No.'

'Tell me.'

'It's just one of those things.'

'Why do you carry it?'

'It's a sort of —'

'Do you carry it when you fly?'

'Yes.'

'A sort of good luck thing?'

'I suppose so.'

'A sort of talisman.'

'That's it.'

A moment later I came back from my eternity of joy to hear a voice hammering out in dead level tones inside me : 'You'll never kill him. You'll never, never kill him. He'll never die,' and so came, at last, to the naked revelation that from now on I too had to believe in the rabbit's foot.

7

So far was I lost in happiness that it wasn't until we were driving home that I remembered the party. Nor had I said a word about the dove-cot.

'Bring some good types,' I said.

'Don't know any. All bad.'

'Bring some really gay ones. I want it to be gay.'

'Let me think. Who could I bring?'

'Matters, of course. And the Count.'

'Don't think the Count could make it. He's gone on leave to find himself a Countess. Terrible, terrible type.'

'What's so terrible about finding himself a Countess?'

'He has three wives already.'

'Pull the other leg.'

'True. He married his way out of Poland and down through Roumania, then into Greece and over into Turkey and then here. Loved 'em and left 'em at every frontier.'

'Fickle man. Perhaps it's just as well he isn't coming.'

'I'll ask MacKenzie and Fitz, for two. Just for contrast.'

I asked who MacKenzie and Fitz were and he said Mac-Kenzie was a Canadian from Winnipeg and Fitz was stinking rich. MacKenzie had a personal war on his hands – it was a case of him against Goering and the Fuehrer. Fitz on the other hand was a man of such delicate and fastidious constitution that he revolted at the mere thought of Mess food and had his lunch sent down by train from the Ritz every day.

'What about girls?' he said. 'Will you need some girls? Mac's got a nice red popsie at the moment. And I think Matters knows a few.'

'Not more than three,' I said. 'I can't have rivals.'

In this happy mood he drove me home, finally kissing me good night while I still sat in the car.

'I love you very, very much,' he said.

I said I loved him too. Then I went on to say that of course he'd heard of people being wildly in love or desperately in love or madly in love or hopelessly in love and all that sort of thing but that wasn't the way I was in love with him.

'What way are you in love with me?'

'Eternally.'

Perhaps it was an over-solemn thing to say but that was the way I felt about it. It was just the way it was.

The following Sunday evening they all drove up to the house in three cars, Chloe, Flight-Lieutenant John Cavendish Fitzroy's dark green Bugatti and a strange yellow and black Rolls Royce whose roof had been sliced off to convert it to an open car. There were six officers altogether and three girls: Splodge, Matters, MacKenzie, Fitz, an Irish boy named O'Connor who reminded me a little bit of Devlin and to my great surprise the Count, together with his Countess. The other two girls were a blonde, heavy-boned hearty named Babs and a sensational copper-haired beauty named Stephanie blessed with a glorious bust, clear green eyes and, as it subsequently turned out, hollow legs.

The Countess was young, dark-eyed, slender, electrifyingly full of nervous energy and altogether very striking. In my innocence I simply couldn't believe that the Count had married her but Splodge said:

'He solemnly assures us he has.'

A few moments later the Count was graciously kissing my hand with no sign of either tension or embarrassment and saying with elegant solemnity:

'My dear Miss Cartwright, I would dearly love to introduce you to my wife, Elaine.'

In the subsequent round of introductions it was John Cavendish Fitzroy who really struck me down. I had never seen anything quite like John Cavendish Fitzroy. If the Count was elegant, Fitz was a piece of impeccable theatrical band-box, all superior six foot something of him. I fully expected him to burst into operatic song. There was a sort of aloof rehearsed poise about him that made you think he was vain, soft, hopelessly spoilt and artificial. His fingers were long and white, the nails so scrupulously manicured that it wouldn't have surprised me at all to have found them tinted too. His hair, a light gold, looked almost as if ironed into place. His neckerchief, pure silk and in a pattern of blue-and-white stripes, was more meticulously knotted than anything a woman could have done and when once he raised a hand to touch a single golden hair into place I caught a glimpse of the inner lining of his tunic sleeve. It was pure silk too and a bright rich scarlet.

I trembled, as I looked at him, at the mere thought of the food Rose had prepared for us. The man who had his lunch sent down by special envoy every day would surely never touch a crumb of our humble tit-bits.

Then, just as I had made up my mind that this impossible piece of male splendour was altogether too much for my mortal world, he did a charming thing. In a voice so unaffected, modest and engaging that I could hardly believe my ears he said :

'I hope you won't greatly mind, Miss Cartwright, but I brought along a small offering to the feast. Will you excuse me while I fetch it from the car?'

Before I could utter my barely audible and astonished word of thanks he was gone and Splodge was introducing me to MacKenzie.

'Joe MacKenzie. Mac to all and sundry.'

'Great to know you, Miss Cartwright. Heard all about you from Squire here.'

MacKenzie, it seemed, called all Englishmen Squire.

'*All* about me?'

'Well, all the best things. You know. Not exaggerated at that.'

I was engulfed in a prodigious smile. My ears were lapped in great muscular waves of laughter. MacKenzie's enormous barrel of a chest expanded with such power that I fully expected to see every tunic button shoot undone. His squashy cap, far more squashy than any other, was stuck far back on his head with a belligerence that was casual, impudent but somehow very muscular too.

I had just finished shaking hands with everyone – the Irish boy O'Connor was so shy that he faded himself out of the picture and had to be dragged in again by Matters, who said 'Paddy, old boy, girls don't bite. I've told you before' – when John Cavendish Fitzroy came back from the Bugatti, carrying half a dozen bottles of champagne, three under each elegant arm.

'Champers!' somebody said. 'Damn good show. Fitz is at it again.'

'Very Ritzy, Squire,' MacKenzie said. 'Very Ritzy, old sport.'

'I do hope you won't mind my doing this, Miss Cartwright.'

'You really shouldn't have –'

'It's a great pleasure and I only hope it will be to your liking.'

After that I led the way up the outside wooden flight of steps to my room at the top of the dove-cot. I was really very proud of my room and they were all loud in their praises of it. I had kept the furnishings as simple as I could in order not to choke it and almost all I had in it were a narrow divan bed, a mahogany corner wash-stand with a pink jug and basin, an easy chair, a few books and a table with my hair brush and powder and face cream and such things on it, together with a pair of silver candlesticks.

All this the men thought was absolutely wizard. Terrific, they said, to have a room of one's own.

'And such enchanting curtains,' the Count said. I still couldn't get over the Count's marital infidelities, just as I couldn't get over a man like John Cavendish Fitzroy belonging to a fighter squadron. It just didn't seem right. 'What flowers are in the pattern?'

'Fritillaries,' I said.

'Quite delightful.'

At this point John Cavendish Fitzroy – I simply couldn't get round to calling him Fitz until some long time later – asked if he might open the champagne. I thanked him and said yes, but if he would excuse me I would go and fetch two or three more glasses.

I had been far too shy to kiss Splodge on his arrival but now the excuse about the glasses took me downstairs and I was over-joyed when he followed me. It had been one of those warm, unblemished days that were so typical of that summer and there was a deep scent of syringa in the air.

After he had kissed me and held me for a few moments I said:

'You won't go when all the rest go, will you?'

'No.'

had never known the presence of any other man, responded with the sublimest concentration.

'Hell, thirsty work, Squire. Any more champagne? Christ, don't say that's the last drop. Squeeze it, boy, squeeze it. Press the tit.'

It was in fact the last of the champagne and I was just about to announce that if anyone cared to have another drink there was gin and plenty of tonics and lime-juice when I heard John Cavendish Fitzroy say:

'Luckily I had the presence of mind to bring a little brandy. Not gin after *that* champagne, Elizabeth dear. Please. It would be like following your darling Rose's celestial jelly with fish-and-chips. Could we find fresh glasses?'

'I'll have gin,' said a voluptuous voice from the bed. 'It always makes me amorous.'

For another hour or more we sat about, drinking John Cavendish Fitzroy's beautiful brandy in the thin light of the two candles. About half way through this Mac sat cross-legged on the floor and played a few tunes on a harmonica and some of us got up and did slow shuffling dances about the floor. I danced first with Splodge, then with Matters and was about to take a turn with the Irish boy when a blonde body cut in and bore him away in savage embrace, clutching him so hungrily to herself that he simply went in silent surrender.

'Leave the man alone, can't you?' a voice said, with such frozen asperity that for a moment I didn't grasp that it was John Cavendish Fitzroy speaking.

My head whoozed a little as I looked round at the party. I had so much wanted it to be gay and now it was gay – beautifully, foolishly, marvellously, divinely gay. If the men were all young gods I felt a little goddess-like myself, my head up in the stars again, my feet dancing. And once as I danced with Matters he said:

'Liz, you look stunning. Blooming stunning. Come out and dance on the lawn.'

'Thank you, kind sir,' I said, 'but it's not on. My feet may be with you but my heart is with Splodge.'

'Bad show,' he said. 'Bad show.'

When the last of the brandy was all gone we started to dis-

'Stay with me a long time.'

By the time I got back upstairs again everybody except Splodge and John Cavendish Fitzroy and myself had full glasses in their hands. When ours too were full I raised my glass and said:

'Well, cheers and welcome, everybody, to the dove-cot.'

'Cheers. Good show. Jolly good show. Thank you for asking us, Miss Cartwright.'

'And that's another thing. Not Miss Cartwright, please, all of you. Liz is the name.'

They all laughed. It was all very jolly. It was going to be, I decided, a splendid little party. Very, very gay. Then suddenly I remembered that no one had ever called me Liz until Bill Ogilvy had done so and in the very same moment I recalled his longing for champagne.

'What lovely champagne,' I said. 'Bill Ogilvy would have liked this. By the way, where is old Bill? Any news?'

For a few moments there was dead silence. It didn't seem, I thought, quite one of those accidental silences that sometimes fall on a company of people when suddenly, for some reason, no one has anything to say. It seemed to me rather a shocked silence and it was Mac who broke in by saying:

'Last news we had was he'd been promoted. Air-Commode or something.' He turned to Matters. 'That right, Squire?'

'Something like that. Too elevated for types like us anyway.'

I saw Splodge give me a quick glance with those unbearably young eyes of his and look as quickly away again. An interminable time seemed to go past before anyone said another word and then the girl named Stephanie said:

'What delicious-looking eats. Somebody must have been standing over a hot stove all day.'

'Oh! I'm so sorry,' I said and hastily picked up a plate of salmon and cucumber sandwiches. 'Do please help yourselves.'

After that the tension relaxed a bit. And I needn't really have worried about the food. Rose had done her splendid best. It was absolutely wizard, the men said. Among other things Rose had managed to get hold of fresh prawns, anchovies and smoked eel and had made a special cream cheese of her own. She had also made two kinds of tartlets, both served cold, one filled with onions and tiny strips of ham, the other with white-currant jelly.

Even John Cavendish Fitzroy, the *gourmet-connoisseur*, was greatly impressed by the white-currant jelly.

'Only once in my life have I ever come across it before. And that was in France, at Chatillon, in the Loire Valley. It takes me right back there. Delectable. Absolutely delectable.'

'I'm sure Rose would find you a pot if you'd care to have one.'

'Care? I'd bless her heart till my dying day.'

Another odd little shadow went across my mind as he said this but it was gone in a moment and I forgot it completely as he said:

'Do give my warmest compliments to Rose. Tell her how divine her cooking is.'

'She'll cry if I tell her that.'

'Tell her just the same.'

Through such trivialities the evening gradually unfolded into merriment. The champagne – I forgot to say that John Cavendish Fitzroy had seen to it, in his fastidious way, that it was well chilled – made us all laugh a great deal and now and then I actually felt it rippling about in sudden cool rising scales inside me.

During the eating and drinking some of us sat on the bed, some on the floor. The Count opened one of the casement windows and sat on the sill, one leg outside and one in, that angular profile of his looking fine and very pronounced, almost god-like, in the setting sun. And perhaps it was the brilliance and angle of the setting sun that continually brought home to me how impossibly young they all looked and that the Count wasn't the only one who looked god-like either. Fresh, gay young gods – that was how I saw them, and not merely from the pleasure of being with them, sharing their company, but every now and then with that slight twinge of shadow.

Presently twilight came on and I longed to light the candles, but when I asked if I could borrow some matches someone, I think Matters, begged me to wait a little longer. 'Sure thing,' Mac said. He had the red-haired Stephanie in gargantuan embrace on the bed, both hands across her splendid thighs.

But soon it was too dark to see and I borrowed matches fr Splodge and lit the candles. 'Bad show, bad show,' M said, 'cramps a guy's style,' and rose from the pleasantries o the bed with a long stretch followed by a frog-like leap that took him stumbling off the end of the divan. 'Christ, overshot,' he said. We all laughed at that and then he got up to draw the curtains.

There were only two windows in the room and as he drew the curtains over the second one he turned and took a long drawling sort of look at the divan.

'Well, hell's bloody bells and kiss my sweet fanny.'

The Count, undeterred by the presence of the Countess, who anyway was sitting in my one armchair on Matters' knee, had taken over Mac's position on the divan, side by side with the red-haired Stephanie, the nape of whose voluptuous neck he was gently caressing with his lips.

'You stinking chiseller. Da-da-da-da! Shoot the bastard down!' Mac said and all of a sudden was in a wild career about the room, in imitation of some crazy dog-fight, in his own personal war. 'Bandits at Angels Thirteen! Press the bloody tit! Da-da-da-da-da! Where is the bastard? Christ, missed him. Hell, where am I? Split-arse turn – watch your bloody mirror! Up! – down now, down four hundred on the clock. How are you, Squire? Watch out, the sods are coming out of the sun. Press the bloody tit – da-da-da-da-da! Brmmmm! Pull out now, pull out, Christ, pull out. You'll be in bloody trouble – watch the rev-counter – one more go – one more burst – press the tit – da-da-da-da-da – got the bastard – in the pissing drink! – piece o' cake! – whack-o!'

We lay about the room in various attitudes of convulsion. The hearty blonde, who was slightly tipsy by now, tried heavy evasive action in face of a swift MacKenzie turn and ended up on her back, legs and short skirts in air, inches of black panties and pale thighs revealed. The young Irish boy sobbed quietly in a corner. With an air of splendid disdain, now more god-like than all the rest, John Cavendish Fitzroy watched as from afar off, smoking a large cigar, leaning against the door. The object of the attack, the Count, continued unperturbed his exploration of the heavenly body on the bed and she, as if she perse in varying degrees of noisy unsteadiness, the only exception being the voluptuous, hollow-legged Stephanie, who had been steadily at the gin for the past hour but who still looked as splendidly composed as if she had done nothing but sleep all that time in sober infant-like peace on the bed.

In the final moments of departure the Count kissed everybody all round, the girls on the hand and then on the lips, then the men on both cheeks. With imperturbable gravity he afforded me the special honour of kissing me not merely on hand and lips but on my cheeks and forehead too. He called me 'dearest, divinest, darling Liz,' declared there was no other like me and that he would be my fond and shackled slave for ever and ever and then departed into the night on the possessive arm of the Countess, who if anything looked more imperturbable than even he did.

At last Splodge and I were alone in my room. The candles were burning down and now and then I saw four of them instead of two. Presently I sat on the edge of the bed and shook my head to and fro and Splodge said:

'All right?'

'Just a wee bit whoozy.'

'Marvellous party.'

'Marvellous.'

Then I found myself groping confusedly back towards the beginning of the party and suddenly remembered the curious awkward silence I had caused.

'Splodge, be a sweet and tell me. Did I put up a black tonight? I mean about Bill?'

'No.'

'What is it about Bill?'

He didn't answer.

'Has he been killed or something?'

It was pretty silly, I suppose, to add 'or something' but anyway it was a long time before he said any more.

'Tell me if he's been killed.'

'The fact is we don't know.'

I asked how it was they didn't know and he said:

'They lost about two-thirds of the squadron in France. They're re-grouping somewhere over here now but a buddy of

Bill's, type named Maxie Spooner, dropped in on us the other day. He saw Bill's kite shot up somewhere over Arras. Looked in dead trouble. Maxie got a lump of tracer in his leg next day and went off to hospital without hearing more news.'

'Does that mean –'

'Couldn't tell where he might land, or even if he did. Panzers were coming up all over the place and there was no real line any more. Everything pretty much of a shambles. Could be a prisoner.'

'You think there's a chance?'

'There's always a chance. I told you before. You can't kill types like Bill.'

I knew you could, but all I said was :

'Let's keep our fingers crossed. Let's hope he was carrying his rabbit's foot.'

'He always carried two.'

'That settles it. He'll come back one day.'

On that self-deceiving note I kissed him good night, then showed him out into the garden and there kissed him again.

'Good night, my precious. Take care of yourself.'

'You bet.'

Finally I was alone in the garden. The gay evening of the young gods was over. The scent of syringa was overpoweringly beautiful and so were the stars. And as I stood looking up at them I listened to the last of Chloe's explosive echoes dying away down the road and it was only when the last of them had gone completely that I started to cry.

8

JULY came in hot and with great beauty. The rambler roses were rich deep crimson with fire. The big-leaved magnolia on the walls of the dove-cot began to show, much earlier than usual, its pointed buds of cream. Every day baskets of fruit came in from the gardens of the big house, strawberries, black, red and white currants, gooseberries and raspberries, and every evening Edna and Rose were in the kitchen, with me helping them, sometimes until midnight, topping and tailing gooseberries, plugging strawberries and making innumerable pots of jam and jelly, including the white-currant one, which in fact turns out in the making to be a pale pink shade.

'We must be sure to save a very special pot for Mr Fitzroy,' I said and Rose glowed with joy that was almost patriotic.

Some time before this, on June 24 to be precise, I had begun to keep a diary. This was directly at the suggestion of my grandmother, who after the fashion of her generation had kept a diary, written in a minute and impeccable hand, ever since her marriage.

'You really should keep a diary. You'll find it of fascinating interest later on in life.'

'Oh! diaries are a bore. Some days there's nothing to say, some days there's too much. In any case you never stay the course.'

'That's merely a matter of discipline.'

'Oh! I'd get bored stiff with it after three days.'

'Moreover we're living in very dramatic times. It seems a great pity not to record what is going on.'

'Dramatic? Going on? Don't make me laugh. What's going on? Entry No. 1, June something or other: *Rose, Edna and I made twenty-one pots of raspberry jam, bottled twelve jars of gooseberries and six pots of red-currant jelly.* Entry No. 2, next day: *Rose, Edna and I bottled twelve jars of raspberries and so on and so forth —*'

'Take my word for it. The war hasn't started yet.'

'To hear Harry talk you might think it was already over.'

Harry, having recovered a first strong flush of zeal, rather like an attack of measles, that had sent him worming enthusiastically on his belly through woods, fields and churchyards, had now entered, like a great many of his countrymen, a strange mood of complacency. Rather like a man who, having been under a dire threat of burglary, suddenly increases his insurance and changes all the locks on his house and is convinced that these emergencies will make him for ever immune, Harry seemed to think that the setting up of pill boxes and road blocks, evacuating sea-side donkeys from beaches and replacing them with mines, sacking Mr Neville Chamberlain and removing all road signs, were measures strong enough in themselves to keep us all safe in our beds for the rest of time.

He found considerable solace also in history, fondly believing that it did in fact repeat itself, and would from time to time remind us over his breakfast eggs how Drake had dealt with the Spaniards or Admiral Hawke with the Froggy fleet at Quiberon or Nelson with the Frogs yet again at Trafalgar. When my grandmother reminded him with gentle acidity of what the Romans and William the Conqueror had done to us and that both had actually camped on the hills not more than three or four miles away, he would say something like :

'Different set of circumstances entirely. No parallel at all,' as if that too solved the problem.

He even became, about this time, rather testy about Churchill, 'The feller tells us to brace ourselves. Well, we brace. And then what? Not a damn thing happens. I tell you, one gets browned off.'

'One of these fine days,' my grandmother would say with that good sense which was so characteristic of her, 'we're going to get the shock of our lives,' and once again would go on to urge me to keep my diary.

So at last, on Midsummer Day, I started the diary, with not the remotest intention of keeping it up. I entered, at first, a mass of trivia : the jams and jellies, the arrival of the first peaches from the glass-houses, the birth of a litter to the Belgian hares. I was excited because a pair of housemartins had started to nest above one of the windows in the dove-cot and I put that in. The

really care for riddles very much and I was getting slightly vexed
– 'Well, the answer's Yes, underlined.'

'Disappointing.'

Then I felt really vexed and said, quite acidly, so that I could
almost hear the echo of my grandmother's voice in my own :

'I do wish you'd stop fooling and teasing. One thing I cannot
bear is teasing. I hate it. Now please.'

'Sorry.'

For the next minute or so I turned away and tried to simmer
down a bit; then I turned my head and saw him grinning. That
made me really annoyed and I was just beginning to think that
this was the asinine way in which quarrels between lovers have
their stupid way of starting when he said :

'This is a mad war, isn't it?'

'I suppose all wars are mad.'

'But this is madder than most, wouldn't you say?'

'What does it matter?'

'People do mad things in war time, don't they?'

'Of course. They're fools enough to take part in them for one
thing.'

'Kiss me.'

'I will not kiss you. I don't like you. I may even give up
loving you.'

'Permanently?'

'Permanently.'

'Which,' he said, 'would be a pity.'

'And, if I may ask, why?'

He then turned and gave me a long, lazy smile.

'Because,' he said, 'I was going to be mad enough to ask you
if you'd marry me.'

I simply couldn't speak. I just covered my face with my hands.
How long I kept them there I haven't the slightest idea but
when I took them away at last and looked at him he was still
smiling at me very gently.

'It isn't a joke?'

'God, no.'

There was no need to say any more. He simply took me in
his arms and we lay together on the grass in absolute silence,
for a long time. When I came back at last some part of the way

hens were not laying quite so many eggs now and I put that
in too. There was a bad accident in the village street in which
a butcher's cart was in collision with an army truck and a
boy was killed and I duly recorded that. I made a record of
several trout, with their respective weights, that Harry caught,
and even of how Rose cooked them.

One evening after tea I was making a few desultory entries
in my little book, which I was holding on my raised knees as I
sat in the window seat of the sitting-room, when my grandmother said :

'I'm glad to see you're persevering with your diary. I'm sure
you won't regret it. May I read what you've written? Or is it
all very, very secret?'

'There isn't a secret word in it. Of course you may read.'

I gave her the diary and for a few minutes she sat reading it
in silence. She had a habit of lightly wetting her thumb as she
turned over the pages of a book or magazine and it always gave
her a rather thoughtful air. She did it automatically as she
turned the pages of the diary and it seemed to make her, I
thought, more thoughtful still.

Finally she handed the diary back to me and said :

'I'm surprised.'

'Surprised? Why surprised?'

'You have all those interesting friends – the young men in
the Air Force I mean – and yet there isn't a single word about
them. I should have thought you'd have been thrilled to record
all the things they tell you.'

'They don't.'

'Don't tell you?'

'It isn't done. It's called a line-shoot.'

'I'm astonished. I thought fighting men loved to talk about
their actions.'

'Only when they're old.'

'Oh? How do you know about that?'

'I don't. I just said it.'

'What did Shakespeare say?' she said. ' "Old men forget." '

'I think young men forget too. I think perhaps they want to
forget. It may be the reason they don't want to talk.'

'How strange.'

A few days earlier she had felt it her duty to invite the Group Captain and half a dozen other officers for a glass of sherry before lunch on Sunday. It was a very formal, pleasantly correct party at which nothing really amusing or exceptional had happened and at which there were just occasional bursts of obedient laughter when the Commanding Officer made such remarks as 'We're trying not to break too many chandeliers in the house, Mrs Cartwright.' The officers were mostly Ad-Min types and of the seven I had met only the Group Captain and the Adjutant before.

Something now reminded her of this and she suddenly said :

'By the way I missed that pleasant young man with those very large moustaches last Sunday. Has he gone away?'

'He was shot down.'

'Oh! my dear. You didn't tell me.'

No : I hadn't told her.

'Was he killed?'

'We don't know. I think so.'

'Why didn't you tell me?'

'I think for the same reason as I said a few moments ago. I suppose I wanted to forget.'

'I see.'

'I suppose it's sort of catching. They don't want to talk and in the end you don't want to talk either.'

She didn't say anything more for a few moments and finally I got up and said :

'I think I'll go for a walk now.'

'Do. And don't forget your diary. And if anything really tremendously exciting happens you will put it in, won't you?'

'I will.'

And with that brief promise I went for my walk, totally unprepared for the fact that two days later the most tremendously exciting event of my life was in fact about to happen.

I rarely, if ever, saw Splodge before ten o'clock at night. His daylight hours were not for me. By that time the pubs were closed but sometimes I got Rose to make me sandwiches and then called in at *The Olive Branch* on my way up to the hills, just before closing time, to buy two bottles of beer, and then

wait for Splodge at the Devil's Spoon, in the last half h[our] daylight. I once heard a flying man say that the most ex[citing] sound he knew was when the prop first turns and the en[gine] roars, but for me, that hot midsummer, the most exciting so[und] in the world was the sound of Chloe snarling up the hill. O[ne] minute I would be sitting there lost, almost drowned, in [the] deep tranquillity of the hillside, where wild yellow rock-ros[es] were dropping their petals everywhere about the chalk afte[r] the scorching day and the scent of wild marjoram was thick on the air where you crushed it, and the next I would be utterly lost, completely drowned, in Splodge's arms. Some of those long hot summer days seemed infinite and I felt like a child who thinks a long awaited party can never possibly begin.

The entry in my diary for that day is a long one and it begins like this : 'Splodge, lying flat on his back on the grass and staring up at the sky, suddenly asked me in a most off-hand way if I knew what day it was. I said I thought it was July 4th and wasn't it an anniversary or something? And he just said "Yes, Independence Day".'

He was quite quiet for about a minute after this until at last I said : 'What was all that about Independence Day? You mean America? It isn't an important day for us, is it?' and he simply said :

'I hope it will be.'

For the life of me I couldn't think what all this riddle-making was about and then he said another odd thing :

'Do you value your independence?'

'Of course.'

'Very much?'

'Of course.'

'Terrifically?'

'What *is* all this about?'

'Would you give it up?'

'Of course I wouldn't. That's what the war's about, isn't it?'

'I'm not talking about the war.'

'Then what *are* you talking about?'

'Independence.'

'And whether I'd give it up,' I said rather sharply — I don'[t] to reality it was still light enough to see his face. For some reason he didn't look quite so unbearably young as he nearly always did. In fact he had become, as he sometimes did, quite solemn.

'Of course I should have to ask Groupie and he might say No. And your grandmother. Oh! good God,' he suddenly said. 'What am I saying? You haven't said Yes anyway.'

Up to that moment my heart had been too full for me to say a word. Now I just laughed and called him my precious and kissed him quickly several times and told him that was my answer.

'You're sure you don't want to think it over?'

'I'm no thinker. I never have been.'

'There's an awful lot of snags.'

'I suppose you snore or something.'

'But seriously, do you think it's mad?'

'Utterly. Absolutely. Barmy. It's the barmiest thing I ever heard of.'

Suddenly I thought that if the conversation went on in this way much longer I should simply end up in tears and I said:

'Tell me, then, about the snags.'

'There wouldn't be a long engagement.'

'No.'

'There wouldn't be any honeymoon.'

'No.'

'I might get twenty-four hours leave. Not more.'

'No.'

'And even after that I wouldn't see you very much.'

'No.'

'I don't make it sound very exciting, do I?'

'Exciting? Oh! God, it's the most exciting thing that's ever happened to me.'

After that we both laughed — I won't say uncontrollably but there was a near-hysterical touch in both of us. We kissed each other madly several times and some little time later he took down the top of my dress and ran his lips across my breasts. It was dark now and in the centre of this wild vortex I once again had the miraculously shining idea that we were both immortal. We were together for all eternity.

'I'll ask Groupie tomorrow,' he finally said. 'And your grandmother too if I can get away.'

After breakfast next morning I wanted to get these stupendous events into my diary as soon as possible and I had just started to write them down in the dove-cot when suddenly I changed my mind and decided to go over to the house instead.

My grandmother was already writing her own diary in the sitting-room. I was aware of a strong tension of inner quietness within myself that morning and I sat writing for more than half an hour without saying a word. I think she herself had been finished writing for some time when I at last looked up and saw her gazing at me with acute and rather amused attention.

'A very long screed this morning. A wholesale order for jam?'

'Read it if you like. I promised I'd put down anything of great importance.'

I gave her the diary and she took it and started to read. For a few minutes I sat nervously watching her face and then all of a sudden I was frightened to watch it any longer. I was mortally afraid she would be shocked or outraged or terribly angry. Any one of these things would have crushed me.

Finally she stopped reading and looked across at me very steadfastly. Her astonishingly bright eyes were always piercing but very rarely tender. But that morning, to my infinite astonishment, they were tender : so much so that I was the one to be shocked.

'I suppose you realize it's like being married on top of a volcano?'

'I hadn't thought of it like that.'

Perhaps my nerves or my shock showed in my face, but anyway she suddenly smiled.

'Don't worry. I'm not going to preach at you.'

'Tell me if you disapprove.'

'I don't think it's my place to approve or disapprove.'

Still nervous, I felt I had to keep to realities and said :

'In any case he has to ask his Commanding Officer's permission first. If he gets that he'll come to see you.'

'Why me? Your mother's the one to see.'

I had utterly forgotten my mother; and now the dithering absent figure came back to shock me yet again.

'Good God,' I said, 'that's torn it.'

She was infinitely amused at that and broke into a big broad smile.

'Would you like me to cope?' she said.

At that I rushed across the room with such half blind energy that I struck my hip against a chair and actually fell into her arms, weeping copiously.

'Splendid,' was all she said. 'Splendid. I wondered when you would.'

Later that morning she had the good sense to send me out for a walk, pretending she needed stamps and a registered envelope from the post office. It was one of those splendidly soft warm mornings that were so typical of that summer and I was wearing my thinnest summer dress. The very slightest variable wind was blowing and now and then a sudden turn of it found its way into the top of my dress, warm on my skin, and I instantly went back to that ecstatic vortex of the night before, when Splodge lay kissing my breasts in the summer darkness and I knew that my conviction that we were both immortal could never, never be shaken. So far, indeed, nothing had shaken it. I was just aware of the loveliness of the summer morning but oblivious of almost everything else. Even a sharp and rather prolonged rattle of machine-gun fire from somewhere down towards the sea did nothing to wake me.

I had just bought the stamps and the registered envelope and was half way down the village street when something happened that did, at last, jolt me out of this fond daylight dream. It was John Cavendish Fitzroy's green Bugatti, standing outside *The Pomfret Arms*. I had never seen it there before.

I stood there for fully a minute looking at it and looking for a sign of Fitz in the street. It was now about half past twelve and finally I decided to look into the lounge of the hotel on the chance that Fitz and some of the boys and perhaps even Splodge might be there.

When I went into the lounge it was to find Fitz sitting at the bar, all alone, drinking whisky.

'Elizabeth.'

It was the brevity of his greeting as much as the tense, bemused look on his face that set me wondering.

'Strange to find you here at this hour,' I said.

'My lunch hour. Didn't want any.'

His voice was brittle; he kept clipping an elegant finger nail against the side of his glass.

'All that lovely food from the Ritz.'

'I've stopped that caper.'

'Really? Why?'

'Bloody silly. Childish.'

This was so unlike the John Cavendish Fitzroy of old that my abrupt conclusion was that he was drunk. In fact he was far from drunk – unless a man can be drunk from excess of feeling, as I later discovered a woman can – and all of a sudden a glimpse of the old Fitzroy came back.

'Elizabeth, I'm most terribly, terribly sorry. I didn't ask you what you'd like. Please, what would you?'

I hesitated, not knowing quite what I wanted, and suddenly he said :

'I tell you what's nice on a warm day. Dry sherry and water and a piece of ice. Would you like that?'

I thanked him and said I would and while the bar-maid was pouring the drink I added that Rose had brought her talents to bear on the new crop of white currants and that she had the most fancy jar of jelly in special reserve for him.

To my infinite surprise he took not the slightest notice of this remark but merely ordered himself another whisky.

Then, when I was less than half way through my sherry, he suddenly struck the bar a sharp blow with the flat of his hand and said 'Blast! Sorry. I ought to get back' and was half way to the door, in his own abrupt oblivious rush, before he just as abruptly changed his mind and came back and sat down and said :

'No good. No, I won't. Sorry.'

This, it suddenly occurred to my untrammelled innocence, was the way men are supposed to behave when crossed in love and before I could think twice about it I said with fatuous stupidity :

'Fitz, you're all on edge. She hasn't jilted you, has she?'

He didn't answer. The joke, poor as it was, passed him by as completely as the remark about Rose and the jelly. Then he started rapidly clipping his finger nail against the glass again, in an acute attack of jitters, and suddenly went off at a complete tangent and said, with some violence:

'I've got this war all wrong. All wrong.'

What this was all about I could only wonder and I had no time to ask before he blurted out:

'Types like Mac have got it sewn up. They're the ones who've got it sorted out. Bing – bang – kill 'em. Blast 'em clean to Hell. No bloody aesthetic cock about them.'

Earlier on I had longed, at intervals, to tell him something of the miracle that had happened to me. I hadn't told a soul except my grandmother and I longed again, as I had done once before, to share the secret with someone of my own generation. But it was no good now and I simply sat listening, in alternate phases of mystification and amazement, while he blurted out fresh disjointed barks of savagery. One of the things that mystified me most was the quite uncharacteristic tone of his voice. It was dark, tortured and at times almost lacerated.

At last he said: 'We had a bad show yesterday. Lost a sergeant and young –'

He stopped. I'd long since learned, or at least partly learned, my lesson about asking questions, and I wasn't asking any now. There would have been no need anyway because suddenly the entire tone of his voice changed, dropping into a key not only low and quiet but completely neutral in the most dead and disturbing way.

'You remember young O'Connor?'

'He was at the party. Yes.'

'He was a very new kid. Hadn't been with the squadron long. He went down.'

There was more than grief in his voice. The lacerated nature of its tone had completely disappeared, leaving it heart-breakingly empty. It was partly his fault, he suddenly said. Spotted him too late, going out on a dice towards France. Didn't think he used his mirror either. Minced him up in no time.

'Jesus,' he said vehemently. 'Jesus.'

Later I talked to Mac about losing friends and he said: 'It's

95

impersonal. No time to think about it. Another name crossed off the slate, that's all.'

But then Mac wasn't in love – girls for him had only one purpose, just as a Spitfire's guns had only one purpose – as I was in love with Splodge and as Fitz had been in love, as it became borne upon my innocence of mind very slowly, with O'Connor. Perhaps the fusion of male hearts is altogether a too complex one for women to understand and the rift that parts them a still greater torment. I don't know. But I inwardly wept for Fitz, in spite of all my own tormenting happiness, that day.

Strangely, as we parted, he seemed suddenly to feel rather better about things, perhaps because he'd been able to talk to me, and at the very last he said :

'Bless you Elizabeth. Splendid to see you. I think you must have thought me a bloody awful cad sometimes.'

'My love to Splodge,' was all I said.

'Great type, Splodge.'

I walked slowly home in the brilliant midday sunshine to find my grandmother drinking a peaceful glass of sherry under a plum tree in the garden and to hear this pastoral heaven broken, five minutes later, by the triumphal brass of Harry's voice, excitedly announcing :

'They got a Hun over the Heath this morning. Lines got the news in the pub. Great big fat fellow. Parachute didn't open. Made a six-foot hole in the ground, they say.'

He actually laughed uproariously but I, faced with the joyful news of the first of our enemies to fall on our village soil, had no word to say.

But my grandmother had.

'From now on, of course,' she said, typically but to my absolute astonishment, 'it's all going to be a piece of cake.'

There were two other incidents I recorded in my diary for that day. Trivial though they may have seemed at the time they have both endeared themselves to me in memory.

In the afternoon I was again overcome by the strong feeling that I wanted to talk to someone of my own generation. I felt I must tell Tom Hudson my news. I hadn't seen Tom since his refusal to join us for a drink at *The Pomfret Arms* and in all the excitements that surrounded me he seemed as remote as the Pole. So that afternoon, about four o'clock, I started to walk up to the farm by way of the river, the strip of woodland that bordered it and the meadows beyond. In one or two fields the wheat already had on it that lovely blue-green bloom that graces it in the weeks before ripening and in the woods the Spanish chestnuts were laden with long blossoming tassels of cream, the odour of them strong on the air. A kingfisher swooped low up the river like a blue and copper scimitar and once I saw a snake swimming across it, darting head just above water.

The Hudsons' big cherry orchard was already completely bare of fruit but beyond it a smaller orchard of plums was laden to the tip of every branch, the plums touched with the first flush of purple. In neither the orchards nor the meadows was there any sign of Tom but in a paddock beyond the orchard of plums I caught sight of his father looking at a foal and its mare. The long slender legs of the foal were sheer gold in the afternoon sun and it ran nervously away when it caught sight of my white frock at the gate.

'Tom's at market,' Mr Hudson said. 'Won't be back till five or after.' He was a big gentle man, one of three brothers who farmed all down the valley, and his hair and moustache were a pleasant mixture of salt and bronze. A less vindictive man it would have been hard to find but his very next words to me were :

'Expect you heard about the Jerry this morning. Just coming out to start milking when I heard this half-tidy rattle up there. So I looked up and there he was, this Jerry, fairly belting down.'

'How did you know it was a Jerry?'

'Saw the plane. Saw the crosses on the wings. I cheered my head off when that bounder came down, I tell you. I cheered my head off. You never saw it then?'

'No, I didn't see it.'

'Dawn patrol I expect,' he said. 'Might have been one of your friends got him, very likely?'

I said I didn't know about that. For some reason I badly wanted to change the subject and suddenly said something about the cherries all being finished so early but what a crop the plums were carrying and how wonderful they looked.

'Never get 'em picked. Short-handed now. Two of my young chaps got their papers last week. That only leaves Tom and me and old Fred and Amos. We'll never get 'em picked.'

After that I said I ought to be walking back and he said 'Any message for Tom? He'll be sorry to have missed you.' I said there was no message and he said:

'If you know anybody who likes a bit of plum-and-apple they're welcome to come and help themselves about a couple of weeks from now. I daresay Tom's mother'll bottle a few but otherwise they'll probably rot on the tree.'

Plums and a fallen enemy: neither seemed, at that moment, of any great importance to me. I was sorry to have missed Tom but that no longer mattered very much either. As I walked back I hadn't a thought for anything or anybody except Splodge and how, that evening, he would come and see my grandmother.

He duly came, about ten o'clock, looking restrained, rather fatigued and by no means as impossibly young as he so often did. When he was tired it was the eyes that went old. A greyness enamelled the blue and the focusing wasn't quite right somehow either. On these occasions the mouth might smile but the mouth and the eyes never smiled together.

I suppose we sat for about twenty minutes talking in a polite and not very serious fashion about this and that when my grandmother, partly I think with the direct intention of getting Harry out of the room for a few minutes, said:

'I think we might have a glass of champagne, Harry. Will you go and get it? The Bollinger '29 if you can lay your hands on it. And get Edna to ice it well, please.'

After Harry had gone out of the room my grandmother sat for fully a minute, in complete silence, looking at Splodge. She was always the shrewdest judge of character and I prayed that the brevity of the meeting with him would have been enough to crystallize her judgement. I needn't have worried, because presently she said:

'Naturally it's not my place to give permission for Elizabeth to marry, but I have talked with her mother.'

'Yes? Thank you.'

'And in spite of the fact that her mind isn't the easiest of minds to make up,' she said in her characteristic fashion, 'she has made it up and says Yes.'

At this point Splodge got to his feet and uttered what were perhaps the most touching words I ever heard him say.

'I should like to thank you both from the bottom of my heart.'

If my tears were very near once more it was again from sheer happiness and I was glad when Harry came back, carrying a bottle of champagne in its silver ice-bucket and followed by Edna with a tray of glasses.

'Well, that was a damn good show one of your fellers put up this morning. Sorry to have missed that. Quite a sight, they tell me.'

Splodge said he wasn't sure it had been one of their fellows but anyway they all counted.

'Oh! too bad. Rather hoped it might have been you. Get a bag today?'

'Not today.'

'Big show hasn't really started yet of course?'

'Not exactly.'

'Think we'll be invaded?'

'Odds on, I'd say.'

By now Harry had finished pouring out the first glasses of champagne. When she raised hers my grandmother simply held it up and looked first at me and then at Splodge and said:

'Bless you both. My fondest wishes for the best of everything.'

At this we all drank and then Splodge came over to kiss me, only to find himself gazing a moment later at my grandmother, on whose face there was a look I never recalled seeing there before: petulance.

'Is the Air Force always so restrained?'

Thus commanded, Splodge went over and kissed her too and she in turn shook him by the hand, her dark eyes brilliantly glowing.

The evening might well have ended on this memorable note but my cup of happiness still wasn't, as it happened, quite full. When I finally walked to the end of the garden, just before midnight, to say good-bye to Splodge I at once looked up, out of sheer habit, at the stars. Splodge looked up too and said:

'You'd better offer up a few prayers for next Friday.' Friday was the day we were going to be married.

'What for?'

'A good thick cloud base. Then all the chaps can come to the wedding.'

I laughed and said: 'You haven't told me who's going to be best man yet.'

'We'll have to take pot-luck on that. Just depends who's available.'

Then I looked up at the stars again and said, after a silence:

'So it wasn't you today?'

'No. My kite's U.S. The fitters have been working on it all day.'

'I'm glad.'

'Why?'

'I didn't want you to kill anybody today – not this particular day.'

He didn't say anything to this but I, with my never quite dormant curiosity, then said:

'I know you don't like talking about it but I've often wanted to ask you. What do you see up there?'

'See?'

'I mean the earth down below and so on. What do you see?'

'Oh! a sort of pattern. Lop-sided. Funny. You're going so hellish fast and sometimes a hell of a way up,' he said and then added the most astonishing thing:

'Of course I see you.'

'Me?'

'Always. All the time.'

'But how? Why me?'

'Oh! you're always there. You're my other rabbit's foot.'

And who could possibly have blamed me if, that night, I went to bed on even more ethereal scales of ecstasy?

9

WE were married the following Friday afternoon, in the village church, at three o'clock. The day was good for flying and as a consequence we were, as they say, rather thin on the ground. Besides Splodge and myself there were only my grandmother, Harry, Edna, Rose, MacKenzie and a young Pilot-Officer named Lambton, whom I had never met before. Hugh Lambton, who had his right arm in a sling, had cracked a bone in his wrist while cranking a car. My mother, mortally in fear as always of the front line, had sent a fifty word telegram, so like a replica of her own voice, and stayed away.

Mac was best man and, like Hugh Lambton, was also *hors de combat*, but not for quite the same reason. Mac had again been conducting his personal war and as a result looked to be one of the oddest best men of all time. His face seemed to have been recently and violently beaten with iron bars. His right eye was very like a ripe purple plum, mauled and vastly swollen, with a sulphur slit across the centre. The other had a livid raspberry hue. Across both sides of his face strips of pink plaster made strange and complicated patterns. His right ear looked rather like a battered lettuce heart soaked in a mixture of stale beetroot juice and oil. His mouth, the lips puffed to twice their size, seemed to have been pushed some inches across his face, giving him a sombre leer. The only other visible signs of damage were his hands, which looked rather like two big battered lobsters.

After the ceremony, when we were all back at the house, my grandmother, never one to show excessive alarm, nevertheless felt constrained to inquire about this extraordinary sight. She hoped Mr MacKenzie hadn't fallen out of his aeroplane?

'Oh ! no, ma'am. Just a fight.'

When my grandmother suggested that it had clearly been fought with clubs, flat-irons or even both, Mac looked as pained as possible under the circumstances and said :

'Oh! no, ma'am. Just an ordinary fight. A plain, ordinary fight.'

'You appear to me to have been at a singular disadvantage.'

'Oh! no, ma'am. Just one of those things. One of those personal things.'

At this point I wanted to know what had happened and Mac said:

'We were just sitting in a pub, having a nice beer, me and Stephanie, when two guys started undressing her with their eyes. That had to be sorted out, sort of. That ain't in my book.'

'Your opponent,' my grandmother said, 'must have been very powerful.'

'There were two,' Mac said. 'Well, two in the beginning. And then later on three. Maybe four.'

'What happened to the others?' I said.

'I think some guys found wheel-barrows.'

'What a shocking affair, four to one,' my grandmother said. 'It must be extremely painful.'

'Oh! just a fight. Just an ordinary fight.'

'Good show,' Splodge said. 'Good show.'

'Good show,' Hugh Lambton said. 'Wish I'd have been there. Good show.'

'Just one of those things, Squire,' Mac said. 'Just one of those things.'

In the evening the six of us sat down to a very good dinner cooked by Rose and that in itself set the seal on my extraordinary wedding day. An hour before dinner was served I went across to the dove-cot to change from my wedding dress – it was a very simple one, in pale daffodil silk – into a long black evening dress, taking my bouquet of white and yellow roses with me. I put the bouquet into the water jug on my wash-basin and then slipped out of my wedding dress. I was still ethereally flushed with happiness, but for a few moments it was good to be alone. Then I kicked off my shoes and took off my slip and stood dreamily looking at the garden outside. Big clumps of white Madonna lilies were in bloom under the crimson rambler roses and on the wall of the dove-cot, just under the window, the first huge chalice of the magnolia was opening, pure and smooth as alabaster.